DEAD IN 10

Chris Danson

ARCACHON

Arcachon Press
www.arcachonpress.com

First published in 2017 by Arcachon Press.

ISBN
978-1-9997695-1-2 (B-format)
978-1-9997695-0-5 (Epub)

For George

ONE

They were the fastest men on earth. They weren't meant to be friends. But what Kane was suggesting was outrageous. They had too much to lose.

As had Trent.

'I'm not doing it, sir.'

He held the phone at arm's length. Kane's voice was too loud. And his flight was at noon. If he'd booked the earlier one this wouldn't be happening.

'A couple of days, max,' Kane said. 'That's all the Germans want. Sit in on their investigation. After that they can do what they like. I'll speak to Masterson. Get you days in lieu.'

Trent flicked on the hotel room TV. The story was still dominating the headlines: Lemond Jackson, the multiple Olympic champion - now more of a brand than a sprinter - and Darius Vondell, the volatile *wunderkind* from Panama. The hype surrounding their rivalry had been difficult to escape that summer, though at this precise moment Trent had other things on his mind.

Footage of last night's race showed Vondell stumbling over the 100m finish line, grimacing and clutching his stomach. Trent felt almost as bad. He had an hour to get to the airport, and a hangover wasn't helping.

Well, Sam, you're only repeating what many others are speculating this fine Berlin morning. The thought that the Olympic champion may have had something to do with this apparent 'illness' suffered by his greatest rival is the stuff of conspiracy theorists. But when the stakes are this high, just a week out from the World Track Championships in London, people will want the truth - and fast.

Clips of Vondell's press conference showed the world record holder ranting at a journalist and repeating his accusation that his drink had been tampered with. He didn't mention Lemond Jackson by name, but he didn't have to. Everyone knew the 'Golden Child' he was referring to. A journalist had also claimed that he'd seen the runners arguing at the warm-up track before the race. The muscular, trash-talking Panamanian had reared up to blow his top, only to sink back into rambling incoherencies about 'someone not wanting him to perform'. It was typical Vondell, who was more likely to be seen with his band of C-list hangers-on than a manager or coach, but this time, curiously, he'd chosen to face the cameras alone.

He sat squat behind a table, hunched over the mic, almost as wide as he was tall, his grey vest slashed in three places. His fierce goatee was similarly unkempt, the stubble creeping up beneath bloodshot eyes. Poisoned or not, he looked ill. Since his world record the press had been keen to paint his rivalry with Jackson as a clash of opposites: Jackson the marketing dream, against Vondell, the fighter from the slums. Trent knew little about their early lives, though it wasn't hard to detect a whiff of xenophobia - racism, even - in the Panamanian's press treatment. Scandal was his steroid. The press lapped it up, but he could floor a heavyweight with his bullshit. With no manager or media adviser to restrain him, he was the loosest of cannons.

Trent moved to the window. Haze was rising above the orb and sceptre crowning Berlin's telecom tower. A great day for sightseeing, for those inclined. But all he wanted was sleep. Sleep and then home. He had a week's leave, and this time he was taking it.

'Trent, you still there?'

'I said no, sir.'

'I tell you,' Kane laughed, 'Jackson's nobbled him. Properly done him over - right before the Worlds!'

Trent gulped some water. It was a Saturday. This sounded like work. And he was now, officially, on leave.

'Look sir, can we talk when I'm back? My flight's at noon.'

'Jackson's running again,' Kane said. 'In the relay. Tomorrow night. The last race of the meet.'

Frank Kane was the only Chief Inspector over the age of fifty that Trent, or anyone else in the Serious Crime Agency for that matter, knew who actually wanted to carry on into their sixties. He was a sucker for it, even with the targets, paperwork, and perpetual rounds of 'performance management'.

He never called this early. Trent knew where things were heading.

'Look,' Kane said, 'we had a call this morning from Zimmerman, the big boss out there - said he spoke to you last night?'

Trent rubbed his face. He'd let the Germans drag him round the Friedrichshain bars after his policing conference had finished early. He hadn't even known the Platinum League meeting was on.

'Briefly,' he said.

'He called Masterson. Said you were boasting about the Stenson case.'

Trent crashed on the bed. The job had been his first in the team, an investigation into tennis match fixing that had seen the young Australian prospect, Wayne Stenson, receive

7

a short jail sentence. A number of European forces had taken an interest in their surveillance techniques, with the publicity a much-needed shot in the arm for Kane's under-funded unit - and Trent's reputation.

'Zimmerman asked for you personally,' Kane said. 'Likes you. Says he wants you around.'

'It's the Germans' turf. Why can't they sort it out?'

'They could. Well, maybe they can. But he said he'd "welcome the benefit of your insight and experience".'

'You mean they don't want to end up with egg on their faces, and you want us to look smart bailing them out?'

The conference had been titled *Transparency and Accountability in International Transfer Agreements*. The young German detectives had been quick to show their naivety, wildly underestimating the more dubious aspects of football agents. They were eager to learn, but just finding their feet.

And this Jackson-Vondell business was risky stuff. Their sponsors were the big beasts you didn't mess with. Sticking your nose into the business of two of the world's highest profile athletes was tempting, but it needed to be handled with kid gloves. They could end up a laughing stock.

'Might look good on a wannabee inspector's CV?' Kane said, riding Trent's hesitation.

'No, sir. I really need this leave. My exam's in four weeks. I'll bomb if I don't prepare.'

Kane sighed. 'Okay. I'll phone *Herr* Zimmerman. Tell him it's a no.'

He rang off. Trent felt like punching the wall. His promotion to sergeant had come swift enough, but getting on was all about looking hungry. Keeping momentum. Results were what got you noticed. The Germans might indeed need a hand, but there was no way he could screw this up.

Besides, he'd be playing catch-up. Only once had he covered an athletics case, tracking down a couple of Eritrean steeplechasers who'd overstayed their visas.

Glamour and big money weren't the rewards of track and field. Not unless you were at the very top. In one way this was good. At least for a cop. Organised criminals stayed away.

He moved to the window. Ten floors down, a group of tourists in the Tiergarten stood fanning themselves at a crossing. A trio had broken off and were arguing. A woman with a map was pointing towards Potsdamer Platz, while two guys inappropriately dressed in raincoats pleaded with her and pointed towards some woodland.

Trent watched more of the news coverage. Jackson's camp had said nothing about the accusation, a calculated gamble, no doubt, given the slickness of his PR set-up. Someone as globally successful as him, both on and off the track, was hardly going to be thrown on the defensive. It wasn't his style. The American was tall and good looking, albeit in a sanitised, shaving ad kind of way. He made a virtue of his temperament, always cool, never ruffled by his rivals' posturing. The idea that he would sabotage an opponent was insane. But he was the sport's highest-paid athlete. He had his image to protect, and sponsors were quick to run.

Accusations aside, Vondell had been doing more than enough on the track to keep Jackson worried. Things had intensified over the past year with the Panamanian producing a scorching run in Eugene, Oregon, where he'd ripped a tenth of a second off Jackson's world-best. Berlin, one of the biggest meets on the European circuit, was the first time the pair had gone head-to-head that season.

Trent looked outside. Sunbathers were taking to the grass, but the tourists had gone.

A stabbing pain gripped his side. He could see the inspector interview panel across the table. Sizing him up. Deciding whether he was the real thing. Or just some chancer who couldn't handle the beat.

He called Kane.

'Just the weekend, you reckon?' He rubbed his side.

Kane laughed. 'So you are up for it, then? That's my boy! Just remember the whisky at the airport - Glen Rosa, okay?'

Trent staggered to the bathroom. A ghost stared back from the mirror. He looked terrible, but it was nothing a big German breakfast wouldn't fix. He was a mug for giving in. He knew that. But it was worth a punt. *Bratwurst* in the sun followed by two weeks at home. And what mug would turn that down?

'This is the last time,' he said, fumbling for an aspirin. *And you can stick your duty free.*

TWO

'Got him. Ten rows up. Above the finishing line. In the shades.'

Trent passed the binoculars to Schönleber, the German detective who'd been assigned as his chaperone. Jackson was slumped in his seat, the hood of his tracksuit hanging low over his mirrored sunglasses. In a move that had further inflamed the press, he'd pulled out of the relay citing cramp, though a sponsor's commitment demanded his attendance at the *Olympiastadion* whether he liked it or not.

'*Ja*,' Schönleber said. 'That's him, alright. Beefed up the security this evening, I see.'

It was almost dark. Huge arrays of spotlights lit the arena, but thousands of camera flashes made it difficult to pick out anyone from where they were sitting, high up on the back straight.

Jackson looked like he wanted to be anywhere else than a sold-out sports stadium, but his minders were doing him no favours. His effort to disguise himself in baggy sportswear was being comically compromised by a gang of twitchy security goons. The only other person inside the cordon was a woman sandwiched between two of the

11

musclemen, late twenties or early thirties, and dressed in a navy power suit.

'Who's the blonde?' Trent asked.

Schönleber looked. 'Ah. Ms Stocking. Lucky guy. Though I guess the world's fastest man - sorry, second fastest - can kind of get what he wants.'

'Who?'

'You mean you don't know Gabrielle Stocking?' Schönleber snorted. 'And I thought you were here to teach me something!'

Trent grabbed the binoculars. She was almost as tall as the six-feet-plus Jackson, with her hair, swept back behind a hairband, accentuating a long neck and stark complexion. On her nose were angular, thick-rimmed glasses. If she wasn't surrounded by 70,000 screaming fans she might be heading up a boardroom.

'Stocking ... the name rings a bell. Wasn't she a model or something?'

'Gabrielle *Leech* was a model. Gabrielle *Stocking* is a business woman and goodwill ambassador. Who is also writing a novel.' Schönleber laughed. 'Though I won't be waiting for the German translation anytime soon!'

Trent remembered now. 'Something about her husband dying ... while waiting for his fraud trial to begin. Didn't they arrest him in England?'

'Ja. Jeff Stocking. Older guy. Made his money in microchip patents. After growing up in England she went to college in Washington to be nearer her father. She caught Stocking's eye while modelling - at some business convention, I think. After he was indicted, the politics around his extradition got messy and she flew to London to be with him. They say she pleaded for him to admit ripping off the other company's technology.'

'I'm guessing it didn't work?'

Schönleber chuckled. 'Wrong. It did work. Once back in the States, he confessed everything as part of a plea bargain.

A week later he had a massive heart-attack. A rich widow at twenty-four - a model's look, but not a model's brain, you might say?'

Trent ignored the smug grin. 'You know a lot about her.'

'Well, ja. She's in the press a lot over here. Hangs with the eurotrash. The magazines love her, what with all her work for global charities, NGOs - that kind of thing.'

A fanfare heralded the climax to the evening. The 4x100m relay squads, a mixture of European nations and an invitation squad of Americans and Jamaicans, were stretching in their lanes. Schönleber picked out the top guys before the first-leg runners were called to their blocks.

Jackson was finally taking interest. Stocking was on her phone, ignoring the track as well as her boyfriend. There was something strange in their body language - almost nothing, in fact, to suggest they were a couple at all.

A burst of movement on the track was followed a split second later by the gun. The French team took an early lead, only to be impeded by the Italian runner dropping his baton. A collective gasp rippled the crowd as the runners hurtled down the back straight. The invitational team, represented on the second leg by one of the Jamaicans, took the lead, only for the runner to catch his teammate napping. A roar greeted the Germans as they forged into contention around the final bend, but their guy was never going to outrun the pursuing American, who overtook him on the straight.

Trent lifted the binoculars. The gangly American was Jad Gaines, who Schönleber had identified as Jackson's training partner at the elite Palm Bay Track Club in Florida. Across the stadium Jackson himself was punching the air, leaping from his seat and barking something as Gaines, all flailing limbs, took the win.

'That seemed slower than on TV!' Trent yelled. 'Or maybe the track just seems bigger?!'

Schönleber was breathless. 'We had them!' He threw down his programme. 'We were coming back. Just another twenty metres!'

'Right.' Trent slapped his back. 'The American was sipping cocktails by the time your guy crossed the line.' He looked over the outfield. Jackson and his entourage were getting up. 'Come on - they're leaving.'

A stroke of luck had come their way earlier that afternoon. An official marshalling the warm-up track had made a complaint about being pushed aggressively by either Jackson or Vondell during their alleged pre-race spat. The questioning officers had concluded there was little in it: the woman was a fantasist looking for compensation, in all likelihood. Schönleber had wanted to go through Jackson's management to question him, but Trent had advised against it. The woman's complaint could be useful - the perfect excuse for floating allegations surrounding Vondell's alleged 'illness'.

They'd catch Jackson off-guard and question him informally. Schönleber would voice the woman's complaint. Though they'd need to tread lightly. If Jackson suspected that a formal accusation of assault had been made, the whole thing could be snarled up in legal tape before they ever got chance. He might even flee the country.

They skirted the pillar-lined concourse. A pack of fans and photographers were jostling Jackson's party.

'We can't take him here, the photographers will have a field day.' Trent searched for an office. 'Can't we move these people on?'

'I'll call security. Split them up.' Schönleber bawled at a guard. The guy barked into a radio. A moment later an officer in cargo trousers and polo shirt emerged from the crowd. He spoke to Schönleber before wading back in.

A whistle sounded. Dozens more security and uniformed police appeared. They hustled the scrum of spectators, journalists and photographers off the concourse

14

and down the escalators.

'My colleague, Krentz, will escort Jackson's entourage to the VIP entrance. There are boxes in the atrium. We'll take him there.' They followed behind the wall of security. Jackson seemed unfazed, sauntering between two giant bodyguards. Behind him Stocking was looking seriously displeased, waving her arms and railing at Krentz.

The security staff peeled off. The uniformed men ushered Jackson, Stocking and the bodyguards into a darkened atrium. Schönleber gestured to Trent. As Jackson reached the next set of stairs they swooped in.

'Mr Jackson.' Schönleber flashed his badge. 'Could you spare a moment, please?'

'What is this, man?' Jackson turned to Stocking.

'Just a few questions, sir. It shall only take a few minutes.'

One of the protection guys pushed his chest in Schönleber's face. 'He ain't got a few minutes!'

Jackson nodded to Stocking. 'Call de Witt.' He pulled aside his minder. 'C'mon fellas, I gotta plane outta here. Learjet's leaking dollars on the tarmac.'

Trent felt the bodyguard sizing him up as he watched Jackson and Stocking. The set-up was odd. She was always six feet adrift, like a consort trailing a king.

A bead of sweat broke on Schönleber's forehead. As the other Germans gathered to block Jackson's way they heard the sound of breaking glass.

'*Entschuldigung!*' A pitcher had fallen from a table. One of the waitresses picked it up. Other catering staff started to appear and were pointing at the standoff.

'I think it would be better,' Stocking said, slipping to the front, 'if we sorted this out somewhere private, don't you think?'

'*Ja,*' said Schönleber, relieved. 'In there.'

He guided Jackson to a smaller VIP box and dismissed all but two of the uniformed officers. The rest of the group trudged into a suite, which overlooked the home straight.

'I should have been here earlier, man. They got candy and everything!' A half-empty bowl of M&Ms lay on the mahogany table. Jackson tipped it over and sloped into a chair. Trent had read-up about his training regime. After a successful junior career, his performances on the senior circuit had stalled, only to be rescued by new training techniques and a gluten-free diet. Vondell, on the other hand, was a prodigious natural talent, who always seemed to come up with the goods despite a fondness for junk food - a fact he never let anyone in his bombastic, often downright chaotic, press conferences, forget.

The suite was smartly furnished, the walls lined with flatscreen TVs. Everything was set up so the great and the good could smash the buffet without ever venturing into the arena. A trestle table was strewn with empty wine glasses, half-drunk champagne magnums and stained programmes with Jackson and Vondell on the cover. A sliding glass door led to a narrow balcony.

'Excuse me.' Stocking strode out, punching numbers into her phone. She had that glow, as if touched by a mystery potion or balm, the same shared by the other celebs Trent had had the fortune - or misfortune - to meet. Despite the aura, she wasn't conventional model material - at least one who'd made her name in the nineties catwalk world of rake-thin clothes-horses. Heads would have turned if she were a road sweeper, though she was handsome rather than pretty, with full lips, a Roman nose and strong jaw. She looked the picture of an ambassador, though goodwill seemed in short supply.

The bodyguards wedged into their seats. Trent tipped his head at Schönleber. 'Get those two out,' he said, quietly. 'The woman too. I want Jackson alone.'

Schönleber whispered in Krentz's ear. They huddled before addressing Jackson's team.

'We'd like you to leave us for a few minutes,' Krentz

said. 'As my colleague said, we want to speak to Mr Jackson alone.'

Jackson laughed. He sank further into his chair. 'I know my rights, man. Ain't gonna happen. Not without my lawyer.'

'It is a small matter,' Schönleber said. 'You shall not need one.'

'What's the time?' Jackson said.

A bodyguard grunted. 'Goin' on 9.30.'

Jackson shifted. 'Look man, can't you just tell me what this is about?'

'Of course,' said Schönleber. 'But it is a private matter.'

'Okay, okay.' Jackson rubbed his face. 'Go wait outside.'

The protection sloped out, eyeballing the Germans.

'This better be good.' Jackson sat up. Despite his laid-back posturing, Trent knew he was sharp. Prior to competing professionally, he'd attended Florida State on a track and field scholarship, graduating with a degree in Business Administration. He'd put the qualification to good use. After the usual golf and tennis megastars, he'd negotiated some of the highest-paid endorsements in sport, appearing in commercials for cars, watches and health insurance.

'This morning,' Schönleber said, 'we received a notice of complaint. From a woman official at last night's race.'

'A woman?' Jackson fell back, grinning. 'Never spoke to no woman but Gabrielle. Signed some autographs, that was it. You can find the fans to prove it.'

'*Ja*. One of the officials at the warm up track. She says that either you or Darius Vondell pushed her. In a manner she felt was aggressive.'

Jackson laughed. 'No way. You got the wrong man. I came out to warm up a good twenty minutes before the race. Go find Vondell. He's the angry dude.'

A chill air blew in.

'What's happening? What have you said?' Stocking stood

with her hands on her hips, her skirt four or five inches above her knees. Were it not for the designer suit and jewellery, she might have been a high jumper or pole vaulter. Her accent, from what Trent could make out, swam somewhere in the mid-Atlantic.

'You got de Witt?' Jackson said.

'He's calling Zimmerman, the Berlin Chief of Police.' Stocking draped her arm over his seat.

'Who's de Witt?' Trent said, pulling up a chair.

'Who are you?'

'Detective Sergeant Trent.'

'You're British.'

Trent smiled. 'Anglo-German police relations. Just here to observe.'

Schönleber whispered in his ear. 'Maureece de Witt. Lemond's manager. Has been since Rio.'

The abrasive South African boxing and Mixed Martial Arts (MMA) promoter had made millions outside the American market, developing his empire in Asia and more recently with East European fighters. Trent had no idea he'd ventured into track and field.

'Miss Stocking,' Trent said, 'we'd be grateful if you'd leave us for a moment. We'd like to ask Mr Jackson some questions.'

'Lemond won't be speaking to anyone. Not without his lawyer.'

Jackson touched her hand. 'It's nothin'. Just some dumb woman at the track.'

Stocking's brown eyes found each officer in turn. 'A woman? They've not asked about Vondell?'

Trent leaned in. 'What about Darius Vondell?'

Jackson jumped up. 'This is wasting me jet fuel, man! Come on, I'm outta here -'

'The media seem to think something else went on last night,' Trent said. 'They're cooking up quite a story.'

Stocking grabbed her Hermès bag. 'Sergeant Trent, can

you explain what this is all about?'

He told her about the track official's complaint.

'And are you planning to charge Lemond tonight, or any time soon?'

Schönleber's eyes pleaded with Krentz. 'Er … we need to see if there are any more witnesses. Other than the journalist, that is.'

Stocking pulled on some white gloves. 'Officer, have you enough evidence to charge Mr Jackson?'

'No.' Schönleber said, fingering a ripped programme.

'Good. So there's nothing to see here.'

Jackson pulled up his hood. He pushed though the uniformed officers.

Trent clenched his fist. They were slipping away. And they'd got nothing on Vondell.

He took out his card. 'Where can we find you?' He grabbed the door. 'If other witnesses do come forward, I mean?'

Jackson gestured at his men. 'I tell you, man, this is harassment! You'll be hearing from de Witt, believe me -'

'It's fine, Lemond.' Stocking smiled brightly, her perfume stinging Trent's eyes. 'We'll be at our apartment. In Monte Carlo. Lemond's training there before London. We also have other business. I don't expect to hear from you again, Sergeant Trent, but if you do want to contact us, I urge you to go through our management next time.' She pulled out her own card, taking Trent's from the table.

Trent opened the door. The bodyguards folded around Jackson and Stocking, giving the Germans daggers as they left.

'*Verdammt!*' Schönleber slapped the wall. 'We should have kept her out of it! As we planned.' He hurled away his programme. 'We scared them off!'

Krentz's phone rang. Trent stepped out onto the balcony. To the west of the arena, staff were dismantling the high jump.

'It's fine,' he lied. It was the Germans' case. There was no point in rocking the boat. 'They were always going to be that guarded. They've a lot to lose.'

'You think there's anything in this Vondell accusation?'

Across the outfield a man with a rake was chasing litter over the sandpit. Trent shrugged. 'Jackson looked relaxed enough. She was just showing us who's boss.'

Krentz reappeared. 'That was Zimmerman. The official's retracted her complaint.'

'What?!' Schönleber spat. 'Why?'

'Gave no reason. We sent people over but she insisted we drop the charge. A fantasist, as we thought.'

'*Nein!* And we were hoping Jackson had caused her some real damage!' Schönleber squeezed Trent's shoulder. 'Sorry, you know I don't mean that. It's just that a proper case would have reflected well on us, don't you think so?'

Trent flipped Stocking's card. He could still smell her. But he couldn't be bitten again. Not with a promotion on the line. Besides, there was nothing sinister here. Catch the early flight and he'd have an extra day's revision.

He tucked her card in his wallet.

It was time to go home.

THREE

'Delayed? For how long?'

He was regretting booking the early taxi. Eager to escape the heat he'd arrived at Tegel airport two hours before take-off.

'Sixty minutes,' the check-in attendant said blankly. 'Maybe more.'

Trent glanced at the terminal clock. It was still only 8.30am.

'Sorry,' the assistant said after seeing his passport. 'Are you *Detective Sergeant* Trent?'

He nodded.

'I have something for you.' She handed him an envelope. On the front was his name, printed in a fancy typeface, the kind used for elderly relatives' birthday cards.

'Who gave you this?'

'I'm sorry, sir, my shift just started. I believe a courier brought it earlier.'

A card inside had the same tacky font. It was an invitation, to the *2nd de Witt Foundation Charity Auction* at the Hôtel du Palais, Monte Carlo, at 7pm that evening.

'Sir, can you confirm that no-one has tampered with

your bag?'

His phone rang. An unknown number. 'Could you excuse me?' He moved to a café. 'Jay Trent.'

'Detective Sergeant. This is Gabrielle Stocking.'

He dragged over a chair. 'Ms Stocking.' He scanned the card again. 'I was just thinking about you.'

She laughed loudly. 'So you got the invite? That's a relief. So sorry for the short notice. I do hope you can come?'

'How did you know which flight I was on?'

'Never mind about that. Lemond and I wondered if you'd like to come to the little charity event we've organised?'

She hadn't expected to hear from him again. He'd believed it. Even if he hadn't wanted to.

'Why invite me?'

'A nice way of clearing the air, we thought, after yesterday's mix-up. Actually, your German colleagues' senior officer suggested it.'

'Who might that be?'

'Carl Zimmerman.'

He grabbed his notepad. 'Go on.'

'The auction won't drag on all night. There'll be plenty of opportunity to meet high-profile guests: sports agents, club managers and the like. Might be a useful networking event for an ambitious young officer? We've an apartment nearby, but I'll be checking in later at the hotel - to oversee things for guests.'

He ignored her over-familiarity and scanned the departure list. The next flight to Nice, the nearest airport to Monte Carlo, left within the hour.

He scribbled down the flight number. Kane would have a fit. Evidence for Vondell's claim was scant at best, but something had driven her to call. Though the sprinters' spat was the last thing on his mind right now.

'Thank you. Then I accept.' He darted towards the

Lufthansa desk. 'Will you be there all evening?'

He waited for a reply, but the line was dead.

By the time he'd cleared security the line of passengers was shuffling towards the gate, though there was still one call to make.

'Hi Claire.'

'Ringing while on leave?! This must be serious.'

Claire Vasey. Shamefully still a constable, despite practically running the shop.

'Listen - I need something.'

'Who is she this time?'

He laughed, in spite of himself. They got on well - very well - but now wasn't the time. 'Can you sort me a hotel in Monte Carlo?'

'Monte Carlo?! You're revising in a casino?'

He explained the invite, but didn't mention Stocking by name. Kane had evidently forgot to tell her he'd been assigned to the Jackson investigation. Then again, Kane forgot a lot of things.

'Hold on.' She spoke with a colleague. Behind Trent a businessman in a powder blue suit stood last in the queue, stocky and tanned, with the bullish, relaxed air of the super-rich.

'You know you really should run this by Kane,' Claire said, choosing her prissy tone. The voice that wound Kane up good-and-proper. The one that almost made Trent fancy her.

'Look,' he said, clocking the attendant's glare, 'my flight's about to close. Tell Kane about what the girlfriend said on the phone. He'll be fine with it, I promise.' He wouldn't. He'd hit the roof if he saw budget being squandered. And if Superintendent Masterson found out …

'Well on your head be it.' She broke off for a moment. 'So we've got the Astoria … the Hôtel de Ville …'

He pulled the invite from his jacket. *Checking in to oversee things.* Get home. Think of your career. *There's nothing to see here.*

'The Hôtel du Palais,' he said, sprinting down the ramp. 'I need to stay at the Hôtel du Palais ...'

FOUR

Darius Vondell was raised in a slum in Casco Viejo, the old quarter of Panama City. After breaking every national junior record from 60m to 400m he'd been able to pick and choose his US college scholarship, finally opting for Michigan State.

Things hadn't started well. Twice in his first semester he'd been arrested after partying in downtown strip clubs. His hedonistic lifestyle hadn't affected his running until his sophomore year, when he'd briefly quit school and flown home after a fall-out with his coach. Persuaded to return, he'd competed on the college circuit in the 100m and 200m, attracting the attention of national coaches with a series of prodigious times. Success on the track was soon followed by growing media interest and - in what proved to be the death-knell for his academic career - a ludicrously inflated ego. A row with a girlfriend had led to an unproven claim of assault, though it was enough to persuade Vondell that the lure of international track and field glory was considerably more attractive than two more years in college.

By the age of twenty he'd quit school. By twenty-four he was world record holder in the 100m, a star fixture on the prestigious Platinum League calendar of meetings, and a multi-millionaire.

Little could be gleaned, however, about his relationship with Lemond Jackson prior to last season. They'd faced each other a couple of times on the junior circuit, with the American, two years his senior, winning both times. Any needle between them seemed to stem from Vondell seizing the 100m record earlier that year. After crossing the line, the Panamanian had continued on his lap of honour, whooping and thumping his chest. Jackson had fumed afterwards about his opponent's rejection of a post-race handshake, in what he'd judged to be a clear and disrespectful snub of an Olympic champion. Vondell had responded in the fashion the world's media had come to relish: summoning a press conference and barking repudiations and put-downs, surrounded by his usual crowd of C-list chums.

Trent shut his laptop. He pushed up the window blind. A thousand feet below, the indigo sea melted into a soft aquamarine, its lighter patches spidered with white. He counted the yachts as the plane banked towards its final approach. Numerous harbours sprouted like matchsticks along the Cote D'Azur. From up here the wealth didn't appear conspicuous, but some of the boats were bigger than his London apartment block: oil sheikhs and Russian oligarchs competing in an exclusive playground, where performance was measured in dollars spent, and there were no rules to the game.

After landing he took the shuttle chopper to the Fontvieille heliport, a mile or so south of Monte Carlo. Behind him, spread out across a double seat, was the blue-suited guy from the plane. Even his aftershave smelt of money. Trent wondered how the rest of his day panned out. A two-hour lunch in the harbour. An afternoon discussing investments with an adviser. A spa, perhaps, before drinks with one girlfriend, then dinner with another.

He arrived at the Hôtel du Palais just before midday. Opulent would be an understatement. The lobby was all marble and running water, with brightly lit cabinets offering all kinds of overpriced junk, from jewellery to monogrammed shirts. He wondered who bought the stuff, then cast his eyes around the ageing playboys, Turkish heiresses and vacationing Eurobond traders. They were already here, sipping espressos on the sun terrace, or downing cocktails in the American bar.

He'd just got to his room when his phone buzzed. Kane had been trying to call. His follow-up text was shot through with expletives about Trent's plane and the hotel. He did, however, confirm that Vondell was booked on a flight home to New Jersey that morning.

Trent lay on the bed and flipped the air-con. There was an afternoon to kill, but he didn't fancy walking out in the heat. He decided on the gym instead. An hour on the machines would give him chance to clear his head. Concentrate on the real matters in hand. Like why the official at the Berlin warm-up track had dropped her allegation without explanation. Or whether it was worth leaning on the Yanks to pull Vondell for a toxicology report. Though it was probably too late for that anyway; if anything had been ingested, it was more than likely out of his system by now.

He made his way up to the roof. An infinity pool stretched beneath a glass arch to the edge of the thirtieth floor. Draped over super-sized sunbeds and cushions like fat velvet cigars was what appeared to be an entire agency roster of catwalk models.

Abandoning the gym idea, he grabbed a towel. As he showered he spied a sliver of shade beneath an arbour. Hi-ball glasses clinked and ice plonked, occasionally interrupted by the lapping of water as the women slid in.

He moved to the guard rail. From this high he couldn't hear the traffic, but it was far from your average neighborhood of honking horns and revving engines - at least not until Grand Prix week. He wondered if any of the models had tickets for Jackson's auction. They hardly looked like sports fans, though the people the PRs liked at these events usually didn't.

Fifty feet below, a path bisected two neat squares of lawn. A couple of seagulls pecked around, the only signs of life. As he panned upwards civilisation began. On the roof of an investment bank lay half a dozen more women in bikinis, splayed out between a nest of satellite dishes. He looked at his watch. Lunchtime. Which probably meant a good two hours up there. He couldn't imagine the same set-up back at the station; the thought of Kane in his budgie-smugglers was simply too much.

That reminded him. Claire needed to sort his return flight.

He was reaching for his phone when it rang.

'Detective Sergeant Trent. I see you're settling in.'

Stocking. He jumped up and scanned the bar. A couple of suits had arrived, prompting some of the women to abandon their towels, but there was no sign of Jackson's girlfriend.

'Ms Stocking. So you're back at your apartment?'

'Correct.' She laughed. 'Well done, detective. Though, I must say, it's rare to see a shirtless policeman.'

He retreated under the arbour. First she checks up on his flight, next she's got eyes on him in the hotel.

She laughed again. 'Don't worry. You can come out now. I'm over here.'

He looked over the edge. A couple of the sunbathing bankers had turned over on the roof.

'No, here.'

Directly ahead, on top of what he'd assumed was another luxury hotel, was a waving figure. He looked through the small telescope on the rail. She was wearing a white swimsuit, cut high above her hips and wedged Roman sandals. The hair band had gone, leaving her hair loose over a large black and gold scarab necklace. Behind her various others, including some of the minders from Berlin, were milling around a pool.

'I thought you'd be at lunch,' Trent said, running the scope over her. 'For the next few hours, at least. Isn't that what you do here?' He scanned the pool beds. There was no sign of Jackson.

She cocked her head. The sun glinted off her silver phone. 'Lemond's out training. He's left me to concentrate on preparations for tonight. I was just ringing to see if you'd checked in okay.'

'You do a lot of checking. That's usually my job.'

Her Hermès bag lay beside her on a table. She swapped phone hands and found a cigarette.

'Yes, well,' she said, lighting it. 'Lemond likes guests to be looked after.'

'I bet he does. High profile charity event. Lots of press. Wouldn't want the great and the good to be associated with allegations of poisoning, mind. Bad for the brand. Though a few million raised for charity might sweeten things.'

'The Foundation's had the room booked for months. I've organised it personally.'

'Of course. Most admirable.'

So she was on the de Witt payroll. He also needed to know where she stood in Jackson's management setup. But that could wait for later.

'It's the coward's way to be cynical,' she retorted. 'That's what my dead husband always said.'

Trent changed the subject. 'So where does Jackson train?'

'Just south of here. The Stade Louis.'

Trent recognised the name. The home of Monaco FC. 'Great stadium. Better facilities than a warm-up track. And big enough for Vondell's ego, too, if he fancies joining in.'

She signalled to a minder. 'He's doing just fine in Berlin

- or back in the States, or wherever.' She drew on her cigarette. 'Look, we didn't get off on the greatest footing - after yesterday's misunderstanding, I mean. I'll get you some more time with Lemond this evening, I promise. He's not at all how you think.' The minder returned with a cocktail. 'By the way, you can't go half-naked. You do know there's a dress code?'

It had slipped his mind. He'd need a suit. Reception would be more than happy to hire one for him, though at some exorbitant cost.

'I'd lend you one of Lemond's tuxedos,' she said, sucking on a straw. 'But he's probably too big for you ...'

FIVE

'Shit the bed!' Kane said, 'what's she playing at?

Trent was calling from the balcony of the American Bar. Kane had already given him the third degree about flying out there in the first place, though his ears had pricked up at the mention of Stocking. A meet-and-greet scheduled for prior to the auction was over-running. Down the corridor the ballroom was still full of kids and parents taking selfies with football players, tennis stars and other celebs.

'I don't know what she's been saying to Zimmerman,' Trent said, 'but he hasn't exactly done us any favours. She pretty much knew everything about our unit.' Kane sniffed. He'd been drinking. In the Prospect of Whitby all evening, Trent suspected.

'Well, I guess he has his reasons.' Kane broke off to order a pint. 'If the Germans know more than they're letting on about this Berlin business, they need to share it, don't they? Stop pissing us about. We're doing them a favour.'

A messy divorce meant Kane couldn't retire if he wanted to. Though with Kane it was never about the money. The unit was his baby, even if the bosses had never seen fit to christen it. Sports Crime Unit (SCUN). Sports Corruption Agency (SCAG). Every acronym had sounded like something spat out by a drunk - or the substances you found in their pockets. After much head scratching, Masterson had kicked the issue into the long grass. It suited her that way. Without a name, their budget was easier to slip by top brass. But things were changing. She needed a win to justify their costs - a big one.

And Kane knew it, too. Kane's Unit. Kane's Outfit. Nobody in the Serious Crime Agency ever called them anything but. And that was fine by Frank. Masterson might give him earache now and again about some-or-other spreadsheet, but she wasn't around to smell his breath at lunchtime. Trent had his own reservations about Kane's drinking, but he also had much to be thankful for. Frank Kane was a better governor than his first boss in CID had ever been. He also had a genuine nose for the work, forging his reputation in the cricket corruption scandals of the nineties. The annual scrutiny of the unit's costs and all the other crap washed right over him. Even if Trent did pass his exams, Kane might still be calling the shots at sixty-five. If Masterson's patience held out, that is.

The piano player struck up some melodramatic tune. Trent watched as the families were ushered out by security. On the concourse the limos were stacking up. They couldn't keep the big spenders - the golfers, the media execs, the Hollywood B-listers - out there for much longer. Not if they wanted their wallets open.

'Look,' Kane said. He was anxious to get off. 'Stay till tomorrow, as agreed. Just keep your ears open. Nothing more than that. Then off to do your homework.' He wheezed. 'And keep your mitts off that bird! They only bring you trouble, believe me.'

'One other thing, sir. I need you to check on Vondell: confirm again that he flew back to the States this morning. I forgot to ask Claire -'

'I texted you this morning.'

'It's just a feeling. Like Stocking knows something we don't. Can you get on to immigration - check that he arrived?'

Kane grumbled. 'It'll have to wait till morning. Just keep your hands down when the bidding starts. I won't be signing off any more damn-fool pledges. My balls'll be swinging from Masterson's Christmas tree if she gets wind of this.'

Trent ordered a beer. He made his way to the ballroom. Reception had relieved him of a king's ransom for the monkey suit, but at least he'd fit in.

He flashed his invite. The doorman waved him though, impassively. He had the standard uniform, right down to the indoor sunglasses, though despite the generic look Trent couldn't help feeling he'd seen him somewhere before.

Almost everything in the cavernous ballroom room was white: the chairs, the stage - even the champagne coolers. Gold chandeliers hung low over tables. The whole effect would have been in keeping with the rest of the opulent surroundings, if it weren't for the ultra-violet spotlights zig-zagging back and forth and turning everything a dirty shade of mauve. It reminded him of a cheap wedding in a pub function room. He thought about winding Stocking up, given she'd choreographed the whole thing, but she wouldn't be in the mood. And he needed to get closer to Jackson, not be pushed away.

The couple were in front of the stage surrounded by photographers. Jackson was in a tux, his hair cropped with a go-faster stripe slashed down one side. The train of Stocking's white ball gown draped a foot behind, her hair pinned up to show off her diamond earrings. There was something stilted in their postures - the way she draped her arm around Jackson make it look like the man was the trophy. In this world it was usually the other way round.

Trent sat by an exit. Stage-right was some sort of exclusive, roped-off area attracting attention from the big-hitters. He stood up for a better look but couldn't see above the security ring. After some announcements the lights went down.

One day, I wish my family would have enough to eat.

The voice was a child's. On the screen a film started-up in slow-motion. A line of families were pictured queuing in a refugee camp.

One day, I wish war would go away, never to return.

A haze of smoke cleared. A boy was weeping. Trent surveyed the line of corporate big shots watching from the stage. Jackson was in the middle. Beside him was an empty chair.

One day, I want to run like the wind.

A throbbing electro soundtrack split the air. The on-screen montage accelerated, revealing more children, this time smiling and racing along a shoreline. Next up, the same group was pictured in a track and field stadium, being cheered on by coaches. Finally, the fastest kid was seen competing on a shiny terracotta track under the glare of a thousand flashbulbs.

'Forty minutes or so. Then we'll be done. We can catch up then.'

Stocking lifted her white nails from Trent's shoulder. Before he could reply she strode down and took her place at Jackson's side.

The final part of the film was about the de Witt Foundation. The charity had been set up by the promoter to help disadvantaged South African children, but 'a growing network of global partners, including food manufacturers and financial services companies, had come on board to help children across the globe achieve their dreams'. The film ended with a shot of the Foundation's sporting ambassadors, Jackson among them, playing soccer with the kids.

... all of this the unique vision of a businessman, sports promoter and leading voice in the fight against child poverty in the developing world. Ladies and gentlemen: Maureece de Witt!

A spotlight came on. The honour guard minding the VIP area parted to reveal de Witt, a cigar smouldering beneath his drooping moustache.

Guests sprang to their feet and applauded, acknowledged by de Witt with the briefest of nods. Surrounded by an arc of Asian business associates, middleweight boxers and girls in heels - who may or may not have been their partners - he looked like a bull walrus leading his herd.

Trent hadn't yet investigated his foray into track and field, or looked into the expansion of his Foundation; from the little he did know, most of his recent promotions had been multi-million dollar boxing events in the States and in the lucrative MMA divisions across Thailand, the Philippines and other Asia-Pacific markets.

Stocking now came to the lectern. *Director of International Fundraising*, her title read. Trent scanned the famous faces as she ran through the bidding rules. The list of pledges brought intakes of breath and wry murmurs of approval. The hottest footballing prospect in La Liga was offering a personal training session at his soccer club's stadium. Jess McGinty, the gold-medal winning Canadian snowboarder seated to Trent's right, had pledged a signed board and a lesson at her home slope. One of the highest reserve prices - $100,000 - was a week with Jackson at the Stade Louis, joining in with his training group and appearing in a watch commercial.

Trent raised an eyebrow. Allegations were still being made against Jackson in the press. Why hadn't he played it safe with something lower key that evening? Or cried off the event altogether?

The first lot was a signed shirt from a World Cup winner. After that came various items of golf and tennis memorabilia. By the time the big money pledges came around, bids were up in the tens of thousands. A day's test-drive of a Formula 1 car sent a wave of laughter around the room when de Witt himself entered the bidding. Going head-to-head against a rival promoter, he finally secured the session for $45,000.

'Not for myself, you understand!' He roared, patting his belly in reference to the car's tiny cockpit. 'For my friend here!'

The room fell about. He wrapped a hefty arm around an Asian associate, who smiled thinly.

The auction finished with Jackson taking the lectern. A cheer went up as he announced that $1.2m dollars had been raised. As he ran through the closing messages, waiters appeared with more champagne.

The bar was strung out along one side of the room. Trent took a glass. He watched Jackson and Stocking give an interview to camera. She did most of the talking, perhaps unsurprisingly, given recent events. Trent didn't recognise either of the journalists asking the questions, but if employed by de Witt or any of his media buddies, they surely wouldn't be too taxing.

As the interview finished, Stocking beckoned Trent over. Jackson stiffened. He called for a drink as Trent approached.

'A credit to the under-privileged, Mr Jackson,' Trent said, offering his hand. 'You must be very proud.'

They shook hands. Jackson forced a smile.

'We made a million.' He took a mineral water from a tray. 'Like we said we would.'

Stocking led them to a quieter spot.

'Sergeant Trent here wanted to apologise,' she said, folding her arms, 'for any embarrassment he may have caused last night.'

Trent waved his hand. 'I'm sure the press will tire of it, eventually. After all, an athlete doesn't reach the top of his

36

game by wilting under pressure, does he Mr Jackson?'

Jackson rubbed his chin. 'You're right. man. I thrive on that shit.' He relaxed. The transition from upright man of business to laid-back self-assurance happened in a heartbeat, though there was something mannered about it all. Trent wondered what he was like in training.

'And the track week with the youngster should be fun,' Trent said. A banker had won Jackson's pledge, immediately donating it to a Namibian girl who'd lost her family in a cyclone.

'Sure thing. Ain't nothing like learning from the best.' Jackson stepped away from Stocking. 'Say man, you know how it is with the media here in Europe. Cooking stuff up n'all. Though I don't blame you for taking interest. Just doing your job, I know.'

'That's right. Just doing my job.'

'You need to catch Maureece,' Stocking said, butting in. 'Before he disappears.'

Jackson smiled. 'I hope we've helped a lot of children this evening, Sergeant Trent.'

'I'm sure you have.'

'I gotta turn in.' Jackson brushed cheeks with his girlfriend. 'Training tomorrow, you know?' He slapped Trent's hand and wandered off towards the VIP area.

A waiter passed. Stocking grabbed a glass. 'First one all evening. How do you think it went?'

'Well, for a charity auction in a room full of overpaid prima donnas … fine, I guess.'

She pulled a face. 'We'd hoped for a million, as Lemond said. There were a couple of big no-shows - footballers, as usual - but Maureece seems pleased.' She revolved her glass. 'I do hope, Sergeant Trent, that you've seen enough to know that Lemond Jackson is hardly the kind of athlete to jeopardise his career over a trivial spat with a rival?'

Trent smiled. There was something funny about the way she tilted her head to the side when making a point.

'Is something funny?'

'No. I'm just thinking. You're very good at what you do.'

Her eyes narrowed. 'Which is what?'

'Being an ambassador. Advocating.'

'You mean telling the truth.'

'I haven't even asked you where Jackson was the night before Berlin.'

She threw back her champagne. 'Your German colleagues had the chance to ask that, but we agreed there was no case to answer. Besides, I invited you here because it might be useful. For your own career.'

'A noble gesture for someone you've just met.'

'It's what ambassadors do. Bring people together.'

'Some might say tonight was just a publicity stunt. Opportunism, after what happened in Berlin.'

She shrugged. 'People can say what they want. As you said yourself, you don't get anywhere by giving in to the press. They create their own fiction.'

Trent remembered what Schönleber had said about her writing ambitions. 'On which you're something of an expert, I hear. When's the novel published?'

For the first time she hadn't a ready reply. 'Er ... September. Early September, I think. Yes. In time for the Christmas market. I'm checking proofs now. Hello!' She pulled over a waiter. 'Bring more canapés. No-one's eating.'

'The title?'

'*A Fortunate Son.*' She fished for a Gauloise Blonde. 'Based on a true story, as a matter of fact. Well, the main character's based on a number of people. You know, as they often are.'

He coaxed the plot from her. A young man returns to South Sudan after studying abroad, only to find his country riven by war. Ostracised from a family that fails to value his education, he embarks on a relationship with an NGO worker - an older Swiss woman.

38

Trent nodded. Who might that be based on, he wondered? 'They fall in love and ...?'

She twisted her cigarette packet. 'You'll have to buy it and find out. Look, I promised to get you in front of people. Come.'

She introduced him to the head of a sports TV channel, who feigned polite interest in Trent's work. All the sponsors hanging about were more concerned in bagging a selfie with a soccer player than making small talk. Others seemed wary of being photographed with a police officer, understandably given the media interest in Jackson, though the storm had lessened somewhat over the past twenty-four hours.

The big stars were beginning to leave when Stocking said, 'I just need to pop to my suite for some papers. Don't head off without saying goodbye, okay?'

Earlier that evening Trent had spotted Juan de Souza sitting with his Argentinian doubles partner, Marcos del Rey, in a corner behind the roped-off area. De Souza had been one of the few fellow professionals to testify against Wayne Stenson, making a locker room of enemies in the process, though he greeted Trent like an old friend. They chatted about the upcoming Grand Slam, before de Souza asked about the Jackson-Vondell story.

'I'm sorry.' Trent put his drink down. 'Excuse me.'

De Witt was lumbering back to the VIP area. Trent shot over and was in front of him before he reached the rope.

'Let me congratulate you, Mr de Witt. An excellent evening.'

'And you are?' De Witt said, his paunch preceding him like a battle tank.

A minder stepped forward as Stocking re-appeared.

'Detective Sergeant Trent,' Stocking said. 'From the British sports crime unit.'

De Witt's jowls moved independently, as if devouring a chop. He shot Stocking a look.

'I trust you enjoyed it, Sergeant Trent,' he said, finally.

'A triumph. Given the circumstances.' The associate for whom de Witt had secured the racing car weekend pushed by with his minder.

De Witt ambled to his chair.

'Do you know, Sergeant,' he said, moustache twitching, 'I have always thought the British justice system the envy of the world.' He beckoned an aide. 'Your work sounds fascinating. Believe me, I would like to hear more about it sometime. But I have business tonight, so you must excuse me.' He thrust out his hand. 'Goodnight, Sergeant Trent.'

His guards moved forward. Trent wondered what his business in track and field really was. If his fights weren't banking enough, things must be desperate.

Before he could take de Witt's hand he was shoved from behind. He tripped forward, almost flooring Stocking.

'Polite fellow,' he said, finding a trio of stone-faced security men now barring the pen. 'Not sure about his friends, mind.'

Stocking looked cross. 'Maureece is an extremely high-net-worth individual.' Her teeth gritted. 'He can't afford to take chances with strangers.' She dragged him aside. 'Look, as I said, Sergeant Trent - Jason, isn't it?'

'Let's stick to Trent.'

'Sorry - Sergeant Trent - I'm sure you've seen enough tonight to understand the kind of values Lemond Jackson represents?'

He had. Or at least he'd seen a script penned by a writer who liked to spin her own story. Though he'd found news items publicising the charity auction stretching back for months. There was nothing to suggest she hadn't been organising it for some time. Whatever de Witt was getting out of the evening, it clearly hadn't just been thrown together to greenwash Jackson's reputation.

'Indeed,' he said, 'but you still haven't answered my question.'

'What question?'

'Where was Lemond Jackson the night before the Berlin meeting?'

She shifted. Fiddling with her dress she said, 'Look, I'm happy to answer your questions, but not here.'

'On the terrace?'

'No,' she glanced at de Witt. 'Too public. I need to finish up some things.'

The light dimmed. A DJ appeared on stage. Dance music started to pump from the speakers.

'There's a lounge attached to my suite. We can talk there, but I need to say goodbyes first. Ten minutes?'

'I was going to suggest the roof bar - another drink, perhaps?'

The earnest look disappeared. She folded her arms. Swaying slightly she leaned in. Her hair brushed his cheek. 'There are drinks at the suite.'

SIX

From what he could see there was still nothing criminal in the Jackson-Vondell fall-out. On the balance of probability. Though Stocking was hiding something. He'd sensed it by the pool. And de Witt was unreasonably defensive, even for a 'high-net-worth individual'.

He could return to his room. Quiz her more at breakfast, before flying out. But she'd hesitated for all of a second before inviting him up.

And the champagne was beginning to talk.

He made his way to the fifteenth floor. Her door was ajar. Inside, a hallway decked with lilies led to three more rooms.

'To your left. In the lounge.'

She was at a bureau, pouring whisky from a tray. Her hair was down again, but she was still very much in character. He wondered why she needed to stay the night there. Her apartment was right behind the hotel.

'Would you like one?' She pushed up a sash window. 'I take it neat, for my sins.' She poured him a glass. 'So,' she sat pertly on a chaise longue, 'finally, you have my full attention.

Trent stepped back into the hall. Through one of the doors a silken bed the size of a helipad stood flanked by a pair of Italian-style tables. The other door, he assumed, led to the bathroom

'Very nice,' he said.

'The staff are amazing. We always have the same suite - it's perfect for these kinds of event stopovers, putting up guests - that kind of thing.'

Trent sat by the window. To the front, a brightly lit fountain dominated the concourse, surrounded by a cavalcade of expensive cars.

'Lovely spot. Exactly the kind of place I'd expect the world's fastest - sorry, second fastest - man to live. The tax incentives are most advantageous, I imagine.'

'We get by.' She kicked off her shoes. 'Though that was a statement.' She pulled up her legs. 'Not a question.'

'I'm intrigued to know where you met.'

'Who?'

'You and Jackson.'

She rolled her eyes. 'A PR function. In Dallas. The perfume company I was modelling for booked me in for a meet-and-greet. A couple of months after Jeff died.'

Trent arched his brow.

'Hmm.' She poured more whisky. 'That's what everyone thought. At least the press had some fun. Though life goes on. "A day looking back is a day wasted". Something Jeff used to say.' She seemed to well up. 'But you can find all that online. God knows I've done enough interviews.'

'So where was Jackson?' Trent got up. 'The morning of the race?'

'In his room. Catching up on sleep. Surely that's something the German police can confirm? The hotel must have CCTV footage?'

'And the day before?'

'Training at the warm-up track in the afternoon, though he must have been in bed before, well, about 9pm at a guess. He likes to act Mr Blasé but gets serious when business calls, believe you me.'

'And you?'

'Same hotel. Also checked in.' She placed a cushion over her ankles. 'You know, Sergeant, this all sounds like basic police work to me.' One of the floor-to-ceiling curtains blew in. She walked over and closed the window. 'As neither Lemond or I are suspects in this non-existent case, one might also see your interest as intrusion.' She whipped away his glass. 'Harassment even.'

Her cushion fell to the floor. Trent picked it up. 'It's strange though, isn't it?'

'What?'

'If Vondell felt he'd been poisoned before the race, surely he'd have had tests to find out.'

'Again,' she topped his glass, 'police work.'

The Germans hadn't pursued it. In truth there was nothing they could do now. Vondell had clearly fingered Jackson, but no official complaint had been filed.

Trent sat on the couch. 'How do they get on, Jackson and Vondell? Really get on, I mean. Aside from all the media crap?'

'Pretty much as you'd expect. Most sprinters aren't exactly best buddies, it won't surprise you to learn. Goes with the territory. All that machismo. Bottled up and unleashed in ten seconds flat. Only one can be the fastest. And that just happens to be Darius - I mean Vondell - at the moment.' She moved smartly across room. 'It's a cut-throat business, as you can imagine.'

'Cut-throat?'

'You know what I mean.' She closed the lounge door. 'Look, I've some real gossip.' She sat beside him. 'You know Marcos del Rey?'

'Juan de Souza's doubles partner? He's downstairs.'

Her smile hung with mischief. 'Promise not to blab?'

'No.'

She raised her eyes to the stucco.

'Ok, I promise.'

'He's doping.'

'Who is?'

'Del Rey.'

'How do you know?'

Her fingers tiptoed over the couch's backrest. 'A guy from Lemond's previous management. Told me, I don't know, maybe eighteen months back? He knew del Rey's doctor - before Lemond signed with de Witt. British guy. Caught him with a needle in del Rey's arm.'

'Could've been cortisone. For tennis elbow.'

'He challenged him. Human Growth Hormone. Doc 'fessed up pretty much right away. Laughed it off like he'd given aspirin to a baby.'

'Why would he do that?'

'He knew the doc would take a bribe.'

'How much?'

'Enough. He never said.'

'And where's this guy now? Your man from the agency?'

She traced a finger down Trent's bicep. 'I don't *know*,' she drew the word out, like he was stupid for asking. 'He's not "our man" anyway. I told you, this was way before we signed with de Witt.'

Trent lifted his arm. Her hand dropped away.

'All this in Argentina?'

She did the head-tipping thing. 'Glasgow. Manchester. Somewhere like that. Del Rey was hating the cold, if I remember rightly.'

Trent puffed his cheeks. This was dynamite. Cheating wasn't his business, though possession of HGH was a criminal offence. At least it was in the UK.

'So?' she said.

'What?'

'What are you going to to do about it?'

Report it to Kane and Masterson. That's what he should

do.

'Forget it.' He reached for the whisky bottle. 'It's history. There's bigger fish to fry.'

'But the doctor - he's a big shot now. Running a cartel. You could make a case.'

'I won't tell if you won't.' He reached for her glass. 'More whisky?'

'This dress. I need to get out of it.'

A Steinway system, stacked like a mini-Manhattan, bookended the fireplace. She turned on some music and went to the bathroom.

Trent glanced outside. Most of the cars were leaving. He bit his lip. He should be doing the same.

A phone rang. He turned down the music and scanned her playlist. Power-ballads. Heartfelt tales of romance. Shrieking divas. There was something touching about her choices, as if he'd glimpsed the fragile canvas beneath the veneer.

The muffled ring continued. He wandered to the table and read the whisky label. Beside it Stocking's bejewelled silver phone lay silent.

The ringing grew louder. It was coming from somewhere down low. He looked under the chaise longue. Nothing.

He stuck his hand into the cushions. Something vibrated. He pulled out a cheap black phone. It rang off. No name. The call list had the same number phoning multiple times that day. There was also a truncated message, from earlier that evening:

you avoidin me wh ...

'Help yourself to another,' Stocking said, coming out of the bathroom, 'or I can call for coffee if you'd prefer?'

He hid the phone. He watched her go into the bedroom, then took out his own. With eyes on the door he took out the hidden phone again and photographed its call log.

'You should probably be going. Unless you've more questions, that is?'

Only the diamonds remained. A pink silk slip had replaced the rest of the evening get-up. Leaning against the door she looked every inch the model, though the way she folded her arms hinted another vulnerability, at odds with her aura. She looked ten years younger, a gift for any photographer, though she seemed conscious of losing more than her clothes.

Trent went to stand but her hand was already on his chest. He ran his fingers up her back, feeling the toned muscle beneath her shoulders.

She eased onto his lap and pushed again. This time he relented. His head hit the cushions, nudging the phone beneath. She kissed him. He couldn't have said anything if he'd wanted to. Which he didn't.

For now.

SEVEN

'Trace it. Get back to me within the hour - I might still be able to catch her.'

Claire repeated back the number. The sterns of the moored yachts looked like cross-sections of luxury hotels. Crew - all tanned, young and beautiful - bounded on and off clutching their morning frappés. Their parties had finished in the early hours, no doubt, but all looked ready to go again.

'Let me see what I can do,' Claire said. 'How did you get the number anyway? Or don't I want to know?'

Trent smiled. A brunette in a swimsuit was laying out on a jetty.

'Is Kane in the office?'

'Not yet. "Transport issues". Again.' Claire tapped away. 'Look,' she whispered, 'you really should be careful. With your exam coming up, I mean -'

He pulled the phone away. She was right, but he didn't need lecturing. Though Stocking had thankfully made the whole thing less awkward, disappearing before he woke. A note on the pillow wished him all the best for his promotion, despite him not mentioning it - at least he thought he hadn't.

He did recall, however, what she'd said about harassment. It had rang in his ears while was rummaging in the couch again for the hidden phone. She was right too. There was still no evidence that a crime had been committed in Berlin. He wouldn't learn anything more from the hidden phone, though: that had disappeared.

'What would I do without your interest in my well being, Claire?'

'Well, yes. As you say, Kane wants a debrief. When he finally rocks up. Can you make it into the office before signing off this afternoon?'

He hesitated. He wanted to get away early. Though the quicker this was all written up and handed over to someone else, the better.

'Ok. I'm on the 4pm flight. Lunch, then I'm outta here. I'll see you later.' He started off towards the beach-front. 'Oh, and get back to me on that trace.'

The bay was bathed in white light. He watched the silhouettes of toppers and jet skis flitting between the luxury hulks anchored offshore. A world of play. Insulated from all the bullshit and stress.

The lunchtime maître d's were emerging outside the restaurants. He ate his *fruits de mer* on one of the larger terraces, trying to figure out why the Germans hadn't pulled Vondell right after the press conference, when he'd seemed to make the allegation, even for just an off-the-record chat. True, he'd made no official complaint against Jackson, but the police were keen enough for Trent to sit in on the interview (or non-interview, as it had turned out), even if Schönleber and Krentz had been more interested in the supposed fall-out at the warm-up track than the alleged poisoning.

A white Range Rover pulled up and disgorged a gang of suits. The men bounded up the decking and headed to the rear of the bar. He wondered what Kane would have made of them. A load of ponces playing big men. Tax-dodging pricks who'd never done a real day's work. Especially the one in the powder blue …

He dropped his fork. It was the suited guy from the 'copter, the one who'd sat behind him on the flight to Nice. He knew where else he's seen him, too: manning the ballroom door, before the auction.

Blue Suit broke off from the rest and went to the bar. The beach side of the terrace was already full. Trent watched the men crowd around a larger table. A couple of six-feet-plus guys with tattoos were carving up huge slabs of meat, egged on by some sharply dressed Asians.

Seated at one end was Maureece de Witt.

Trent threw down a bank note. The drink might have numbed his anger at his manhandling last night, but it was all coming back now.

He skirted the other side of the bar, edging between a Middle Eastern family and some ladies-at-lunch. The Asian guys - Thai or Malaysian, he guessed - saw him first and pointed. One of the East Europeans, shaven-headed and dressed in a vest and shorts, jumped up and shouted something in what sounded like Russian. His biceps and facial scars suggested membership of de Witt's MMA stable.

'I want to see Mr de Witt,' Trent said, pushing by.

'De Witt no wanna see you.'

A thick arm striped with scars barred his way. Blue Suit shot over and whispered in de Witt's ear. A group of excited children had broken away from their parents and were gathering beside the South African, as if awaiting a puppet show.

'Sergei!' De Witt bellowed, noting his young audience. 'Let our friend through. Come on!'

The second East European looked up from his steak. He spat gristle at Trent's feet.

'Hardly Monte Carlo manners,' Trent said. 'You know your friends really need to work on their hospitality.'

The South African raised the crab claw he was dismantling. 'You must excuse Nikolai's table manners, Mr Trent. He prefers cracking heads to lobsters.'

The others roared. Blue Suit pulled over a chair. He jabbed it into the back of Trent's legs.

'Will you join us, Sergeant Trent?' De Witt said. 'I think we owe you an apology for last night.'

The fighters returned to their steaks. The Range Rover guys and the Asians - de Witt's guests from the previous night? - pretended not to watch.

'My men here were over-enthusiastic in doing their job,' de Witt said, jabbing a fork at Trent. 'I neglected to tell them you were a police officer.'

Trent gripped his chair. There was something maddening about such a naked apology. Though de Witt was one of those sports management svengalis who spouted bollocks on tap.

'It's fine,' Trent said, accepting a sparkling water. 'I won't be filing a report. Though I might ask to see your Russians' visas.'

De Witt's knife wobbled over a tomato. 'You know Sergeant,' he bellowed, 'I had you down as a joker when we spoke last night. Truly I did! But in a good way, you know - a man who knows how to enjoy himself. I like that.' He shouted for more wine. 'You'll not have something stronger? The Saumur here really is first-class.'

Sunbathers were taking to the sand. The sight of the women ignited an argument between the Russians, who started to fight over some binoculars.

'Thanks, but no,' Trent said. 'Never on duty. Well, almost never.'

'Ah yes,' de Witt said, 'the department you work in - sports investigations or something?'

'Sports corruption. Athletes doing bad things. Or people doing bad things to them.' He ran through a selective history of the unit. De Witt grunted after each mouthful,

51

raising his eyes only when Trent mentioned Wayne Stenson.

'Ya, a talented boy. A shame. Really it was.' He wiped his mouth. 'You know Sergeant, there's something I want to do for you. As my personal apology for last night.' He gestured to Blue Suit, who dropped a black suitcase on the table. De Witt took out an envelope. 'Here I have two tickets for the Drey-Bashin fight. Ringside seats for you and a guest. It's back in Munich, though I hear flights are cheap.'

Trent sipped his water. The light heavyweight clash was the biggest on the boxing calendar. Hype had been building for months after Ezekiel Drey, the American champion, had finally agreed to defend his title against the Belarusian Alexei Bashin. Ringside tickets would be changing hands for thousands. But he was forbidden from accepting gifts. Ones that size, at least.

'I find track and field more stimulating,' Trent said, resting back. 'At the present time.'

De Witt put down his knife. His balding pate was the same hue as his lobster.

'By that I presume you are referring to this nonsense with Lemond Jackson, ya? You know, it is unfortunate when athletes resort to this kind of slander. It really can do some damage to the reputation of an honest competitor.' The waiter arrived with the Saumur. De Witt took a mouthful and spat it out. 'It's bloody warm! Where the hell's it been, man? Get me a chilled one, for chrissake!' He ripped off his napkin. 'We have good people thankfully,' he said, returning to Trent. 'To manage all this. Protect our brands.'

'So has what happened in Berlin damaged Brand Jackson?' Trent had caught the morning papers. The innuendo had disappeared from the back pages but still lingered inside. Stocking, he assumed, was one of de Witt's 'good people'.

'This "scandal" you speak of,' de Witt said, '- it is not

something we recognise.'

'You know one what else I'm wondering?'

'Yes?'

'Why all this is worth your while.'

'What?'

'Track and field. Surely the boxing's the real cash cow? This lot too.' Trent nodded at the Russians.

'Schalk!' De Witt shouted something in Afrikaans, prompting Blue Suit to return. 'I was just offering Sergeant Trent tickets for the Drey-Bashin fight.' He locked fingers over a swollen belly. 'However, it appears that my generous offer has been declined.'

Schalk slammed the case shut. Tattoos bulged on his forearms. Despite the slick attire he looked more than capable of handling himself. As, apparently, de Witt's senior protection, he might have even been a fighter himself.

Trent continued 'I'm also intrigued as to why your employee would go to such lengths to invite me to your charity auction *gratis*, when ordinary mortals are asked to stump up thousands for the privilege.'

A phone in the case rang. De Witt answered it, knocking his chair over as he stood.

'Kak!' He turned away, only to recoil at the gathering children. 'Ya,' he spat. 'No! What do you mean?' He lowered his voice. 'Here now, ya. Out on a flight today you said. I thought that was this morning?' He ripped the binoculars from the Russians. The rest was inaudible as he combed the beach.

He hung up and gathered his men.

'You know, Sergeant Trent, I believe it is now my liberty to ask you some questions. The name of your superior officer in London, for example?'

'I'm sure you can find out. Technology's a wonderful thing.'

'We don't do technology.'

Trent felt Schalk at his neck. 'Then I'm surprised this

one can't help you.' He thumbed behind. 'He followed me from Berlin, after all.'

One of the Russians snatched Trent's phone away. He tossed it to his countryman. De Witt ambled over to the kids and handed a boy the binoculars.

'Just don't point them at the sun,' he said, patting the youngster's head. 'You might get burned.' He sat again. 'Give the officer his phone. If he won't answer me our business is over.'

The Russian thrust the phone into Trent's stomach. He doubled over. When he staggered to his feet his face was inches from Schalk's blue lapel. The cloth was pilled, he noticed. Nothing like the quality he'd imagined.

'Goodbye, Sergeant Trent,' de Witt said, returning to his meal. 'You'll have to watch Drey-Bashin on pay-per-view. It's the closest you'll get to seeing me again.'

The ring of muscle closed. There was no rope this time, just an arc of pulsing necks and deltoids.

Trent started back to the hotel. Like Stocking, de Witt was hiding something. He could feel it. You didn't throw a thousand-dollar ticket a cop's way without expecting something in return. Like him keeping his mouth shut. Whoever had just called, de Witt had promised them that Trent would be flying out that morning. It had to be Stocking. Though surely it hadn't been her idea for Schalk to trail him on the flight from Germany? Not after she'd come onto him quicker than Jackson from his blocks.

Another super yacht was mooring up. The *Crystal Swan*. Trent strolled down the jetty as the crew fired ropes onto the walkway. Above them a well-fed guest in chinos and a darts shirt looked on intrigued from the sun deck, as if he'd discovered some blessed relief from cruising.

'She really is something, isn't she?' a voice said. 'Though who could afford to keep her, I wonder?'

'Schönleber! What on earth are you doing here?!'

The German was sitting on a bench facing the other

direction. Fifty yards ahead, the sunbathing brunette Trent had spotted earlier had found a patch of sand.

'Where are their men, I always ask? You never see them on the beach together. Never!' A copy of *L'Equipe* lay on Schönleber's knee. He prodded it in the woman's direction. '*Ja*. But I wager you she has one. The best ones always do!'

Trent picked up the paper. A small article had a photo of Stocking and Jackson beaming at the charity auction, but there was no mention of Berlin.

'Sorry to - how do you say - "step on your toes" - but *Polizeidirektor* Zimmerman sent me over to keep an eye on our famous promoter, Mr de Witt, over there.'

'Isn't that why I'm here?' Trent dropped the paper. 'Zimmerman arranged it. He spoke to Kane - my boss in London.'

'*Ja*, well. They never tell me anything.'

'Sorry?'

The woman on the sand was adjusting her bikini.

'I said they never tell me anything.'

Trent sank onto the bench. He'd been getting somewhere, even if there was nothing in the way of hard evidence. Having a novice like Schönleber around would only make things harder. The botched questioning of Jackson proved that. And if the letch ever got near Stocking …

The woman on the sand turned over. She glanced disdainfully over her sunglasses and returned to her book.

'You see the way she looked at me, just then?' Schönleber tugged Trent's wrist. 'Like putting up a wall of steel! You'd need a Swiss bank account just to get her number.' He chuckled. 'Getting back into de Witt's lunch party would be easier.' He gestured across the bay.

'You saw me there?! Why didn't you come over?'

The German reached into his bag. He took out some sandwiches. It looked like his mother had packed them.

'Well,' he said, taking a mouthful, 'I'm told Maureece de

Witt meets lots of people. It's easier to see who comes and goes - from sitting here, I mean.' He stuffed some more sandwich in and sauntered to the yacht. '*Ja*, still there,' he said, peering between the rigging. 'Though I only have two hours more. Do you know they asked me to stay on for four more hours in total? My flight was meant to be at two o'clock. Another thing they didn't tell me!'

'A Range Rover pulled up. Do you know those guys ?'

'Hmm ....' Schönleber glanced over his shoulder. 'Not really. The tough guys in the vests are fighters, Russian I think. Pretty sure the suits are Thai. They were at his charity thing last night.'

Trent grabbed his arm. 'You were there too?!'

'*Ja*, of course.'

'And you saw me?'

One of the Russians turned. Schönleber pulled up his hood and sidestepped behind the *Swan*.

'*Ja*. Well, I arrived somewhat late. As I said, it was all short notice.'

'Why didn't you say something?' Trent said, no longer hiding his irritation.

Schönleber grinned. 'You were sitting near Jessica McGinty, *ja*? Well, don't say anything to Zimmerman, okay, but me and my brother were *totally* in love with her when we were younger - posters on the wall - everything! I just had to introduce myself. "Hello, my name is Erik Schönleber of the Berlin *landespolizei*, and I just wanted to say that I was your biggest fan when growing up in Karlsbad ...."' He smirked his way through an embarrassing tale of teenage infatuation. 'When it was clear she wasn't eloping to the Black Forest with me, I moved on. Next thing I saw you had gone. Did you even get to speak to Lemond Jackson at all? Or that phony bitch Gabby Stocking?'

'No.'

Across the water de Witt roared with laughter. The

South African's entourage joined in, rippling and bobbing like the front row at one of his fights.

'Saw them on the stage,' Trent said, 'I got a migraine when Stocking stood up. Left soon after. All the travelling, I think. Jetlag catching up.'

Schönleber's gaze drifted back to the sunbathing woman. He sighed and removed his hood. '*Ja*, well. I guess many men get headaches thinking about her. I know I do.'

Trent looked at his watch. He'd said enough. His German colleague seemed to have done a piss-poor job of watching de Witt. And he didn't want any more questions about Stocking, for obvious reasons.

'What's happening back home?' Trent said. 'In Berlin - did anyone keep tabs on Vondell? Until he flew out?'

Schönleber shrugged. 'You know the woman who withdrew the warm-up track complaint? So Krentz offered her a meet-and-greet with Jackson, though how he got that from Jackson's people I have no idea. Might look like an admission of guilt, no?' He fished in his bag for his thermos. 'But what do I know, right?'

They parted. The real story here was about Vondell's accusation, not the nonsense with the woman official beforehand. Trent would need Schönleber's statement on what had happened at the *Olympiastadion*, but that could wait until he returned from leave.

He jogged back to the hotel. The snake of super cars around the fountain had been replaced by taxis. A pair of guards stood at the top of the stone steps watching the road. Despite the lack of activity there was something forbidding about the gilded edifice, as if he'd been permitted a glimpse of a world he'd never see again.

He was thinking about doing what he'd promised he wouldn't - texting Stocking - when his phone rang.

'You didn't pledge your inheritance away then?!' Kane's cigarette-stained cough wrestled its way to a laugh.

'Sir, Schönleber - the German - is here. Why didn't you

tell me he was coming?!'

'First I've heard. If that slippery bugger Zimmerman bothered to return calls, I might have done. Anyway, we might have a lead.'

'On what?'

'That flight. The one Darius Vondell was meant to catch. Only he never caught it after all.'

'The Americans said so?'

Kane cackled. 'Didn't have to. Crazy bastard's turned up here in London. Charged with wrecking a room in some boutique hotel - whatever the hell that is - just this morning. He's at Charing Cross police station. The press are all over it.'

'You're having a laugh?!'

One of the hotel guards had come down the steps. He watched Trent while fingering his cuffs.

'And you ain't gonna believe this.'

'What?' Trent paced around the fountain.

'That number you got Claire to trace. You'll never guess who it's registered to.'

'Go on.' Trent peeled his shirt from his chest. He had an inkling. He just didn't want to hear.

'*Mr D.M.J. Vondell.*'

EIGHT

'Trent, J.'

'Sorry, sir?'

Trent sighed. He slapped his pass on the sensor once more. 'Jay Trent. Sports crime. Specialist Crime and Operations.'

The machine burped a two-tone raspberry, like he'd given the wrong answer on a gameshow.

'Ah - I apologise.' The security guard pointed at the screen. 'It appears you're listed as Jason.'

Trent clenched his jaw. Outsourcing had seen Murdo, the grumpy Scot who'd sat there for twenty years, packed off into retirement. Kane had organised his send-off in the Prospect of Whitby, a right-royal knees-up, where Claire had told Trent he was the best-looking guy in the station. Despite never marrying, Murdo had never been short of bad advice about women himself. Watching the clueless contractor fumble for a temporary pass, Trent found himself missing the old bugger.

It had gone 7pm. The ops rooms was busy for the end of the day. Busier than he wanted it.

He found Claire working with the guys on the horse-doping case, but he was in no mood for a chat.

He sloped over to his desk.

'Where's the chopper then? On the roof?!' A booming voice jerked the room into life. Kane thundered in, catching a desk with his thigh, almost spilling his coffee. 'Ouch! You still reckon he's nobbled him, then? And that bird, Trent, don't tell me ...'

He stank of it. It wasn't the 1980s. You couldn't do this any more. And Frank Kane wouldn't, not if Masterson or any of the top brass ever set foot in there.

'Tried to call when I landed, sir,' Trent said, hunching over his screen. 'You didn't answer.'

'It's a Monday, Jason. The day after the weekend. A man needs time to adjust.' Kane launched into his rendition of *Suspicious Minds*. The same old routine, though Trent couldn't help worrying what some of the new guys - the smug Welsh kid Priestland, for instance - made of it all. Or what they might be saying to their mates across SCO.

'Sir,' Claire said, sidling over. 'Redstone's at Breton's. He's made some headway.'

'Brittany? What's he doing in France? Booze run?'

'The stud farm, sir. Breton's. In Kent.' She had her back to Trent's face. That was annoying him too. 'He's managed to get a statement - from the horse trainer's wife.'

Kane pulled up a chair. 'Well, well. Ambitious little toe-rag ain't he? You'd think he had inspector exams to prepare for.' He jabbed Trent's seat. 'Where you should be now, my son.'

'You asked me to stay in Berlin.'

'Damn it!' Kane finally spilt his coffee, adding to his shirt stains. 'I did.' He fumbled for a paper towel. 'But *Herr* Zimmerman called me after hearing about Vondell and this hotel business. Papers are writing it up as "overpaid star loses and takes it out on a trouser press". By the wonders of technology we know differently, of course.'

'Don't you see?' Claire said. She sat on Trent's desk.

'They're having an affair. Gabrielle Stocking - she's sleeping with them both.' She crossed her ankles, swinging them back and forth like a schoolgirl.

'So,' Kane said, tapping Trent's knee, 'you can get back to your books. Good way of winding up your rival though, ain't it? Shagging his missus. Hardly a criminal offence, mind.'

'Where's Vondell now?'

'Training. Well away from the press, if he knows what's good for him. He'll get a rap for trashing that poncey hotel, but he won't be up before the magistrates until after the Worlds.'

'He's moved to Stadium Park,' Claire said, tossing Trent a newspaper. 'One of the corporate hotels.'

He checked the back pages. A photo from last night showed Vondell storming out of a restaurant in sunglasses and a tight pink t-shirt, the neckline low over his muscular chest. In another life he might have been a media mogul or an *enfant terrible* of the fashionati. But trouble would follow him anywhere. He was that kind. Despite the world record he still played the underdog, something that made Trent instinctively warm to him over Jackson.

Though at this moment he hated them both.

'What about Maureece de Witt?' he said. 'I left you a message. He's bent. We should check him out.'

Kane swiped the paper. 'On what basis?'

'Do some digging. Those Russians he has around. The Thai entourage. Hardly your standard track and field set.'

'Globalisation, Jason. Just because some rich Saffa fancies earning a few extra quid on the back of some show-pony, it don't make it a crime. Besides, we ain't got budget for "digging". We've got horse dopers to catch.' Kane shut the paper, a smirk spreading over his wind-slapped face. 'Actually, what we're all dying to know is what you got up to with Lemond Jackson's girlfriend.'

Claire walked away. Hearing where Kane was heading,

the others leaned in.

'So what's she like then?' Kane said, his smirk widening. 'This Gabrielle Stocking? Interested in the unit is she? We could give her a tour.' He thumbed over his shoulder. 'Introduce her to the cream of British manhood.'

Trent squirmed at the laughter. 'Explained her work,' he said. 'The charity stuff. I wanted her to tell me more about Jackson and Vondell - their relationship -'

'Let me guess: she didn't want to tell you? And I think we now know why!' Kane guffawed. 'Well, it's a good job you found that phone of hers. You might have made a right tit of yourself.'

Trent had resolved to keep his mouth shut, despite the sniggering. Spilling the beans wouldn't be in anyone's interest. On the flight back he'd managed to convince himself that Jackson and Stocking were a relationship of convenience, cooked up by their publicists to further their media profiles, though the theory hadn't made him feel any better at all. She could do as she wanted - as any man would, any night of the week. She was a free agent.

Even so, he felt like a mug.

'Well then,' he said. 'I won't bore you any longer.' The write-up would have to wait.

'Suit yourself.' Kane returned to his racing tips. 'Then again, you've had your freebie for the year. No doubt we'll paying for it for as long. Could have been a decent case, mind, what with the Worlds coming up. Say, Priestland, you swung those tickets yet? Start-finish straight, you said?'

The air was sharp with copier fluid. The smell and the aircon were giving Trent a headache. He was knackered. Back to the apartment for an early night, then a week's revision. Just as he'd planned in Berlin. Though that was when making inspector seemed the most important thing in the world.

Claire caught him as he walked out. 'Trent - that book you once mentioned - the promotion crammer. New edition. Hinton in Extradition's got it. Said you can borrow it.'

'When I'm back.'

'Won't that be too late? I could drop it round.'

'Yeah, and when you dropping round my Glen Rosa?' Kane barked. 'You pick it up or what?'

NINE

'You've reached the phone of Gabrielle Stocking. If your enquiry concerns my ambassadorial work, please contact Annette Montand on 377 89 56 78 23. For press, modelling and all other enquiries, please contact de Witt Management ...'

Trent slammed open the bi-folding door. He walked onto his decking. The sun's glare bounced through the maze of Docklands high-rises. His phone felt like a hot coal in his hand. Where the hell was she? He'd left three messages already that morning.

He cracked open a beer. The apartment had cost an arm and leg, despite him only owning half of it. The public servant scheme had been his ticket out of the whole flatshare game, though his father had been quick to brag to half of Colchester that his son owned some swanky pad in London. Though he'd been lucky - luckier than some of his mates still scratching around in Essex. He sometimes wondered what his mother would have made of it all, seeing him now. He'd worked hard for it, she'd tell him. Deserved it. Though never get above yourself. That way you're heading for a fall. He didn't believe a word of that last bit now. But she'd meant well. And she'd done for more than his father ever had to make it happen.

That reminded him, it was her birthday soon. He should put flowers on her grave.

His phone rang. Beneath it his revision notes lay untouched.

'I'm revising, Claire.'

'Glad to hear it.'

He threw back his beer. 'Tell Kane I drank his whisky. Bumpy flight. Shitting myself. Had to be done.'

She laughed, like a man, the way she always did.

He laughed too. 'Seriously, I'm on leave. What is it?' Not another bloody book. He hadn't read the ones he'd got.

'I've news. On Mr Vondell.'

He walked in for another beer. 'No-one's bothered. You heard Kane.'

'Look -' Claire lowered her voice, 'this is going to fly - if the papers pick it up -'

'Get back to your horse doctors. You've got a case.'

'He's been papped. In Hyde Park. With a woman. It's trending.'

Trent put down his bottle. 'What woman?'

'Who do you think?'

'Gabr -' He checked himself. 'Stocking.'

'It's all over social,' she said, soberly. 'Check what he's wearing. Lame disguise didn't work. You'd think he was in enough trouble from wrecking that hotel. Really, you have to wonder what she sees in him.'

Her tone teetered on prissy. Trent put the beer back in the fridge.

'Claire, I'm revising for an exam. The best you, Kane or anyone else can do, is try and let me pass the thing.'

'I was just -'

'Goodbye, Claire.'

He found the image on his phone. Vondell and Stocking were sat under a tree, a dawn jogger blurring past. Stocking had made no attempt to keep a low profile, wearing a fur collar and boots like stilts. Vondell was in a puffa jacket, a beanie hat and sunglasses. The half-light made his identity plausibly deniable, though enough people were naming Vondell and Stocking to make it news.

He switched on the TV. There was nothing on the sports networks, at least not yet. Vondell had originally been booked on a flight back to the States to prepare for the championships - a trip he'd abandoned to hole up early in London and take his anger out on a Shoreditch hotel. That was an offence - but he'd get away with a fine once the Worlds were over. As Kane said, seeing your main rival's girlfriend behind their back wasn't illegal, however angry Trent felt about it. If Vondell had planned to meet Stocking in England, it meant Jackson must still be in Monaco.

He grabbed his coat. Her phone might be switched off, but he wanted an answer.

He just wasn't sure of the question

TEN

'No, sir. There's no-one staying here by that name.'

Trent searched the receptionist's poker face. Stocking might well be travelling under an alias. 'Or Jackson. She might have checked-in under Jackson.'

The woman typed away. 'No. I'm sorry, sir.'

He trudged out onto a traffic-choked Park Lane. That ruled out the Four Seasons, Grosvenor and the Dorchester. That left only the Hilton and Verdana Spa.

A siren made him jump. An unmarked car came hurtling round from Hyde Park Corner, only to get stuck behind a crawling coach. Trent ducked beneath the trees. This was ridiculous. There were enough officers around to be onto him in minutes if a bellboy reported some weirdo out celeb-stalking. Though he could always blame Claire. Frank might even be sympathetic: rules were for fools. Unless they damaged the unit. Fuck about with that and you'd be straight back on traffic duty. And sticking your oar into the business of the biggest sprinting star on the planet - off duty to boot - was a sure-fire way of getting the unit ditched for good.

The Verdana was impressive, but not a patch on the

Hôtel du Palais. The lobby centrepiece was a raised glass fishpond stocked with koi carp. A young boy was leaning over the edge throwing in stones from an orchid pot, the son of an oil sheikh or construction magnate, perhaps. The hotel had undergone a change of ownership but looked half-dead, despite boasting a Michelin-starred restaurant and infinity pool.

He asked the same question. The pair of east Europeans on reception looked at each other and shook their heads.

'Are you sure?' Trent scanned the marble desk. A scribbled name. A letter. Anything to suggest Stocking was staying there.

The boy yelped in delight as a fish thrashed to the surface. Unable to contain himself any longer, one of the concierges stormed over. As he was telling the boy off Trent noticed a group of men sitting in a recess. There were four of them, all playing with their phones. Bored. Waiting for something. It was then he noticed two broadcast cameras on the floor.

The press pack.

He wandered over. In his bag was his lanyard from the Berlin conference. He turned the photo to his chest and put it on.

'They arrived ?' he said to no-one in particular.

The oldest guy eyed him up and down.

'Yes, mate,' he said gruffly. He clocked Trent's lanyard. 'Where you from?'

'Multisport. Social media.'

The others looked up. One of them had an Arsenal cap beside him on a seat. He was a photographer - Trent recognised him from soccer matches he'd policed. The older guy he'd first spoken to - a tabloid hack by the looks of it - frowned and gave a half-nod. He had no idea what Trent was on about. Though his gamble had worked. Maybe. They were waiting for someone.

Trent picked up a copy of the *Mirror*. The back page had

a short report about Vondell's bail conditions, but no picture. A couple of inches were given over to the rivalry between the two sprinters, but more space was devoted to the other key showdowns at the Worlds. The heats of the men's 100m were scheduled for the Friday, with the semis and final the following evening.

The concierge was still remonstrating with the kid. Behind reception his colleague glanced nervously at the press guys. Trent fingered his lanyard. He'd been told no once before. He could only be told no again.

He strolled back over. Leaning on the counter he lowered his voice. 'Look, I know the person I'm looking for, Ms Stocking, is staying here, so why don't you just ring up and tell her that her friend - Jay Trent - is here, hmm?' He flashed his photo. If he hadn't done anything wrong until then, he sure as hell had done now.

'Wait with the others,' said one of the concierges. 'Though I still need to speak to my manager. None of you should be here.'

'Jay - Jason - Trent. Just call up. She'll want to see me.' She wouldn't. Though neither would she want him hanging around the lobby like a bad smell. Not with the red-tops sniffing around.

The other concierge returned. The pair argued in Polish before one said, 'What is your organisation again?'

'Multisport.' Trent buried the first syllable. 'But I'm also a friend, as I said.'

'Sorry, your name is?' A bead of sweat stung his forehead. He almost said "sergeant".

'Wait please.'

The more nervous of the two picked up the phone. It rang for an age before someone answered.

'I have a Jason Trent here for you.' He repeated Trent's name, then went quiet for thirty seconds. 'No ... yes, alone. Yes, of course.' He spoke in Polish to his colleague.

'Suite five, floor seventeen,' the other one said, finally.

'The penthouse.' Trent made to leave. 'And sir, if you haven't left by twelve we're to call security. Their instruction.'

The lift was a jewellery box of mirror and gold. Trent saw he had the beginnings of a beard. He peered in closer but had to turn away. He looked like his father.

He walked onto the seventeenth floor with a sense of déjà-vu. Like Monaco, he'd had a drink. Though nothing would happen. He'd promised himself that. He was too angry. Say your piece and get out. Back to the real world. Back to your books and your godforsaken exam.

Her door was firmly shut this time. He knocked once. Someone moved inside. He knocked again. There was a rush of steps before the door flung open.

'You've done your job. Just leave us alone.'

Standing in the crack of the door, in running tights and a stars-and-stripes vest, was Lemond Jackson.

ELEVEN

Trent rocked back on his heels. So they *had* flown in together.

'I'm sorry. I assumed Gabrielle -'

'A cop don't assume.' Jackson's face was daggers. 'Not where I come from.'

'But Gabrielle. I thought she was here?' Trent looked down the corridor. Jackson never went anywhere without minders, but there was no sign of them here.

'Why?' Jackson said. 'You spoken to her?'

'No, I mean, I've been trying to.'

'About what?' Trent bit his tongue. It was a good job Jackson hadn't checked her missed calls. Though who knew how many phones she had?

'I just wondered if she'd seen the news.' The door opened further. There was a large balcony. On a glass table was some lurid juice or shake.

'What news?' Jackson spat. He seemed to be alone.

'It would be better if I came in.' The Lemond Jackson from the *Olympiastadion* returned. He stood tall, his head nudging the door frame, his black eyes penetrating Trent's phoney lanyard and everything behind it. The look that had lesser athletes beaten in the callroom.

'The press are downstairs,' Trent said. 'They know someone's here.'

Jackson looked down the hall. He glanced both ways before letting him in. Trent could smell his sweat. If he'd trained that morning he must have flown in last night. For the first time he felt the power of the American's physique, his own body tensing at what he was about to say.

'Gabrielle was photographed,' Trent said. 'This morning. In the park opposite. With another man.'

Jackson's face remained still. He waited for more. When Trent didn't offer any, he turned and sauntered to the table. He put a hand on his phone, then slid his fingers across to some keys. He was masking his reaction. But the slumped shoulders said it all.

'So what?' He went onto the balcony. 'She must have been out running. She does that too. Trains - like me.'

'In a thousand-dollar coat and heels?'

Jackson spun around. 'Look, man,' he picked up his phone, 'all that shit in Berlin ... we're done. No case to answer, just like they said. Now what you want with Gabby anyway?'

Trent scanned the suite. A pile of giant holdalls and suitcases lay unopened by a large L-shaped sofa. A trail of sports gear led to the bedroom. No woman would stand for that. If they'd travelled together, Stocking wasn't here now.

Trent took out his phone. He showed Jackson the photo. The American breathed sharply, but didn't look away.

'Look,' Trent sat down, 'we know she's having an affair. With Darius Vondell. Is that what Berlin was about? The scuffle with the official?'

Jackson gripped the guard rail. He looked over the park. 'What else you know?'

The lanyard was burning Trent's chest. 'I'm a police officer. We know lots of things.'

Beside the drink - some kind of vegetable juice - were Jackson's Louis Vuitton sunglasses. He thrust them on and moved back around the balcony.

'Fuck up's gonna cost me medals. And money.' He jabbed a finger at Trent. 'But what that bitch done ain't no crime!'

'So you do know.'

Jackson pushed off the guard rail. He slunk into a chair. 'Yeah, I know.'

Somewhere in the park a child shrieked. Trent caught the tattoo etched under Jackson's tricep. Beneath a picture of a Native American it read *Give me the eyes to see and the strength to understand.*

'So what happened in Germany, at the warm-up track with Vondell: the bust-up was real?'

Jackson picked up his drink. 'The woman dropped charges. Nothin' happened.'

'Something did.'

The American rolled his glass in his fingers. 'Prick was in my lane. He set me off. I'd warned the dumb fuck before about messing with Gabby. He didn't listen!'

'And the official - the woman?'

'Got pushed over. Trying to intervene. She never got hurt or nothin'.'

Trent walked to the edge. 'What about Vondell's illness?'

Jackson sat up. 'The punk lost. All-ends-up. I don't know nothin' about no illness.'

For all his big-race temperament and business acumen, Jackson evidently had a short fuse. But there was little to be gained in lighting it. He was a victim, however hard it was for Trent to see him that way. And besides, he hadn't risked his badge coming for him. He wanted Stocking. For what, he wasn't entirely sure. Though something about the setup stank, beyond their sordid triangle.

The sun was bringing on a headache. He was regretting the beer. 'Can I get some coffee?'

Jackson glanced warily at the clock. It was 11.45am.

'Keep the press dogs waiting?'

'Sure.'

They stepped inside.

'When did you land?' Trent said, sitting at the breakfast bar.

'Say man, is this gonna go straight to the media? 'Cos I ain't sayin' another word if it is! You're only here 'cos you helped me and Gabby out.'

Trent didn't understand the comment. He wondered what Stocking had told him.

'Of course not. You have my word.'

Jackson sized him up and down, as if pondering a watch endorsement. 'Yesterday evening. Learjet.'

'I thought you were staying in Monaco? To train?'

The coffee maker glugged to a halt.

'Yeah, well. That's before she disappeared over here. Now half the world knows why.'

'The hotel's been helpful - they usually like decent notice before some big shot rocks-up.'

'Booking's in her name. Has been for months.' Jackson passed him the coffee. 'Milk?'

Trent turned to the window. For a moment the craziness of the situation hit home. Sitting in a penthouse overlooking Hyde Park. Being served coffee by one of the most famous sportsmen on the planet.

Whose girlfriend he'd just slept with.

Jackson walked into the sun. 'Told me she was coming here - to work out, as I said. Wouldn't tell me what else she was up to, though it wasn't hard to guess - not after Vondell got busted.'

'So you knew she was here?'

'Her press agent's in Knightsbridge. Bond Street's a cab away.' Jackson sipped his drink. 'How else she burn my money so quick?'

Trent glanced at the stack of Fendi luggage. Surely she

didn't need Jackson's millions. Not with Jeff Stocking's fortune and a modelling career behind her?

Over in the park some teenagers were stretching out by a fountain. The girls kicked off their sandals, self-consciously adjusting their skirts before lying back. It was a good job Schönleber wasn't there.

'So Gabby and Vondell - how long's it been going on, if you don't mind me asking?' Trent heard another police siren. They were making him paranoid.

'Yeah man. I do mind. 'Cos it's none of your fuckin' business.'

Trent stiffened. He sipped his coffee. When he looked up, Jackson was grinning.

'But I'll tell you anyway.' Jackson removed his shades. Trent realised now what Stocking saw in him, beyond the fame and fortune. He needed to share. With no manager, coach or entourage there to scaffold his ego he was lost. The Vuittons were armour - against rivals, the press and the doubters. She was the same.

'Boston. Last indoor meet of the season. They hooked up there.'

Trent flipped a mental calendar. Back end of February, early March at the latest. A good six months ago. 'But you're still together?' He asked it like a question.

Jackson sipped his juice.

'You've kept it from the press,' Trent added.

'We've got good people.' Jackson eyed Trent's phone. The photo of Stocking and Vondell shone from the screen. 'Well, we did have.' He sat back, his long legs splaying like a crane. 'Wanna try some?' he said, noticing Trent eyeing his juice. He pushed it over, ignoring his own phone, which was ringing.

'What's in it?'

Jackson laughed. 'If I had a dollar for every time I heard that.' The olive drink was flecked with white and had leaves floating in it.

'I'll stick with coffee,' Trent said.

'Wise man. Can't be sure what athletes consume. Not these days.' He flashed his teeth. The giant elephant that was drugs had long since busted out of the locker room to park itself inside every stadium and warm-up track on the circuit, though Jackson had always avoided the worst of the innuendo. The same couldn't be said for Vondell, who'd come under greater scrutiny since his world record. He lacked Jackson's Corinthian profile, or the same "good people" to look after his image, though media prejudice was as much to blame.

'You're not splitting up then?'

'Finish your coffee.' Jackson retrieved his phone. 'Even if we were, it ain't gonna happen before a major championships. Can you imagine the shit on our profiles?'

'So that's what you and Gabby are all about then? Profile?'

Jackson listened to a phone message. The voice was male. 'I gotta go train. Say man, where's Vondell holed up now?'

'Dunno.'

'I thought cops knew things.'

Trent walked inside. 'Good coffee.'

'Let's hope he don't do to her what he did to that hotel.'

Trent stepped over some kit. 'I almost forgot. What's the real reason you invited me to your auction? Not purely in the interests of my career, surely?'

'Er ... de Witt,' Jackson rubbed his forehead. 'Hospitality. Yeah - he likes to spread it around.'

Stocking had said nothing to that effect. 'Ah yes, Maureece de Witt. When did he take over your management? There must be something in it -'

Jackson shot a look at the clock. 'Time's up.' He ushered Trent to the door.

'My pass.' Trent's lanyard was on the balcony. He'd need it for what he had planned.

'Do me a favour,' Jackson said, following him out. 'The press - if they don't know I'm here, just keep them waiting, okay?'

'Sure.' He'd do no such thing. He'd be taking the tube to Stadium Park. One of the corporates, Claire had said. There were two hotels he could think of. Three at most. And if she wasn't there, a certain other sprinter might well be.

The sun had disappeared, casting a grey film over the park. As he leaned over the table something flashed by the fountain.

'What is it?' Jackson said, seeing Trent stop.

A figure sidestepped behind a tree. They appeared again. Another flash.

'Someone's taking photos.'

Jackson went to say something but stopped. 'Fuckin' …' he searched for the word, "paparazzi!"'

Trent dropped to his haunches. He raised an eye above guardrail. The figure had come further into the open. It wasn't one of the teenagers, the man was too stocky, his torso filling his t-shirt like a bag of walnuts. Neither was it a press guy from downstairs.

Jackson shot inside. He stuffed a holdall full of gear.

'Time's up man. You gotta go.' The US team were based at a college in north London, he explained. He usually arranged his own training facility, but this time he'd agreed to train with his buddy Jad Gaines and the rest of the relay squad.

'You haven't told me about de Witt.'

Jackson pulled on his team hoodie. He grabbed Trent by the lapel.

'Whoa!' Trent shrugged him off. 'Remember who you're -'

'Sorry man, we're done.' Jackson steered him to the door. A damp film covered his brow.

'I thought you had muscle for this stuff?!'

'They're checking de Witt's security detail ... before he

77

flies in.'

Trent stuck a foot in the door. 'Which is when?'

The glass table in the kitchen shook, the trill from Jackson's phone vibrating it like a jackhammer. Trent waited for him to answer, but Jackson stood there open-mouthed, like he'd seen a ghost.

TWELVE

'Step away, sir, or I'll have security remove you.'

'I'm a friend, as I said. Now if you'd just ring up -'

The receptionist picked up the phone. 'Should I call the police?'

Trent pushed through the throng of Vondell fans, reporters and angry guests queuing to check in. The Welcome Rest's duty manager was waving his arms around, miserably failing to orchestrate the crowd. It was evident Trent's lanyard trick wasn't going to work here. It also didn't take a genius to realise that the World's Fastest Man was in the building.

'Move back! Please, can you all move back!'

A woman with a French accent was shouting. She was by the lift, wearing a cream trouser suit and holding a clipboard. She looked stressed, her die-cut cheekbones rose-white.

'Gabrielle!' A photographer sprinted over. Stocking emerged from the lift, head bowed. She looked smaller than Trent remembered, despite her heels. Then again, everyone was the same size in bed.

She turned up her collar and slipped on over-sized

sunglasses. Flanked by the Frenchwoman and a pair of skinny groupies - twin brothers, they looked like - she made her way smartly to the exit. Most of the tourists seemed to be wondering who she was. Only the photographer and a journalist bothered to follow.

The concourse fanning out from the mall was filling with lunch-goers. As Trent gained on the group a party spilled out from the transit hub. Stocking tried to go around, only for a child with a balloon to run up to her.

'Mummy! It's Gabrielle Stocking!'

The mother rummaged in her handbag for a notepad.

'Ella's such a fan,' she said. 'Me too: your style, all the great work you do for charity ...'

Stocking glanced around as one of the male assistants searched for a pen. Trent came over and stood, arms folded, behind the mother. On seeing the young girl, the chasing media abandoned pursuit.

'Ella, you say ...' Stocking signed her name. 'Well, you have a great -' She saw him and froze. 'Well, Ella, you have a great day.' She snatched out her gloves. 'Annette, we're late.'

Trent stood motionless. The mother and daughter skipped off. The French woman, Annette, looked at him blankly, but there was no hint of suspicion.

He followed them into the mall. At one point Stocking stopped and seemed to go the wrong way, only to be directed up an escalator by one of the brothers.

Trent called her number. She stared at her phone, then turned discreetly. Seeing him again she hid behind her hair, like a schoolgirl keeping a secret.

'You look lost,' he said, still twenty yards back.

'No, no,' she said loudly. 'But our business is finished. As we agreed.'

Trent laughed. 'Business? Is that what you call it?'

They walked onto the upper level. White-faced mannequins in designer gear gawped from window displays.

So this was how she shopped.

'Yes,' she smiled at Annette, now looking concerned, 'that's right. And no, I don't think we need to speak again.'

'You've ignored my calls. Why?'

'Have a great day. Goodbye.'

'I don't rate the Verdana penthouse. They let anyone in.'

She stopped and searched the domed ceiling. 'As I said, goodbye.'

'Surprised there's time for shopping. What with de Witt arriving.'

She moved to a shop window.

'I asked Lemond when the flight lands,' Trent said, 'but he wouldn't tell me.'

A dummy reclining on a sand dune was being repositioned by a window dresser. Stocking leant against the glass.

'Okay, well ...' She turned to Annette, who was tapping her watch. 'Perhaps I could find time.'

'A chat. That's all.'

'There's a personal appearance I'm late for. The new wellness clinic by Staves.'

A cream carpet was being rolled out by Staves department store. Assistants in white scrubs were running around balancing urns of lilies on plinths. Others were struggling to blow up gold balloons. Standing bored by the entrance were two bronzed male models wearing nothing but trunks.

'Lunch then?'

'I'm having lunch with my press agent -' She looked to Annette, who mouthed something. 'And then I've a meeting in town. At five.'

'Hyde Park?'

She turn to him. 'No. Clerkenwell. A girlfriend.'

He scanned a mental map.

'3pm. Mick's café on Lamb's Conduit Street.'

'Lamb's what?'

81

The twins were muttering to one other.

'Lamb's Conduit Street,' Trent said. 'Ask your hipsters. They'll know the place.'

THIRTEEN

The last of the late lunchers were drifting back. Trent ordered a slice of Efe's apple cake, his favourite when studying. That and Mick's Pie of the Day. The smell of oil and toasted sandwiches brought back all those afternoons wondering what he was going to do with his life. He'd been sitting at the same table when a girlfriend had persuaded him to fill in his police application.

Above him the Cyprus-shaped clock said ten past three.

'So this is where you're hiding.' She stepped down into the tiny back room. They were alone apart from an old guy reading a paper. 'Can we make this quick, please? I've got something at four.'

She still had on the coat with the collar up. He understood she needed to lay low. But she was hardly Jackson- or Vondell-famous. Then again, being papped in a greasy spoon would be gold dust for the magazines, despite Mick's fine cuisine.

'Summoned by the boss?' Trent said, eating some cake. 'Which airport's he landing at?'

The walls were plastered with autographed celeb photos. She raised her eyes disdainfully around the pictures of soap actors, sportsmen and reality TV stars, many squeezed in between a beaming Mick and Efe. Tightening her coat, as if fearing catching something, she said, 'Why were you at our hotel?'

'Our hotel? The room was booked for one.'

She took out her phone, the silver one he remembered. 'Why are you following me? I could have you fired.'

If she was sweating on the pap shot of her and Vondell, she wasn't letting on. Though she must have seen it. Her "people" would have told her.

'You know your boyfriend really is a decent guy. Behind all the posturing.' He wanted her to say "which one".

'You can't be harassing Lemond,' she said. 'The Worlds start in five days.'

He offered her some cake. The corner of her mouth twitched. A smile slipped out, despite her best efforts.

'Suit yourself,' Trent said. 'Why didn't you answer my calls? I must have tried twenty times.'

'I've a busy life.'

'That's right. So busy you're meeting Darius Vondell at dawn in Hyde Park.'

She sat up.

'The photo's everywhere,' Trent went on .'And you talk to me about upsetting Jackson's training!' He tore his napkin. 'Lemond knows you're having an affair. I know it. Now the world knows it too.'

'Look, sergeant.' She clasped her hands. 'I'm photographed every day of my life -'

'Must be inconvenient. Screwing-up again. Right before a public appearance.'

She pushed aside his plate. 'I understand it might make you angry, Jason, but I'm more than capable of fielding sticks and stones. You don't get to my position without a thick skin.'

He stretched his legs. 'So you're not denying it?'

She checked her phone. 'Is that what this is about?'

'I just think -'

'Who I see is my business. I'm sorry that our fun in Monaco has blown up into something quite different in your mind, but I don't remember promising more.'

'How long's it been going on? Seriously, I'm trying to help. You know the press over here - they could be right outside.'

She rolled her eyes.

'Lemond told me everything,' he said. 'All that bravado … seems it's all for show. He's a far more sensitive guy -'

She raised her hands. 'Okay! Okay! Yes, something's been going on between me and Darius Vondell.' She snatched up her bag. 'But that's for me and Lemond to sort out. Now can I go, please?'

Trent called for some water. He should never have boarded the flight to Nice.

'I need to meet him.'

'Who?'

'Vondell.'

'I suggest you return to your real work, sergeant -'

'I didn't catch him in Berlin. Just a few questions. You know, enquire after his health.'

'He's in your justice system. After his,' she drew inverted commas, '"error of judgement".'

True. But getting an interview would mean sign-off from on high. And that wasn't going to happen. Not today. 'It's better if you arrange it,' he said. 'Simpler all round.'

'No.'

She got up.

Mick arrived with a jug. 'More coffee, Jay?'

'Please, Mick. And she'd like -'

'Nothing.'

'So you're off to meet de Witt?'

'Excuse me.' She got up.

'You should call Lemond. He's terrified of him.'

She took a backward step. Something on the wall caught

her eye. 'How sweet! He sent a message to Maureece and Alexei - wishing them good luck for the fight.'

It was a faded picture of Danny 'Scud' Simpson, the middleweight-turned-trainer.

'Who's Alexei?'

'Alexei Bashin. He's fighting for the world title -'

'Yes, yes, I know,' Trent snapped. She sounded like Claire.

'Where I should be now. Goodbye.'

Trent was miffed. 'I thought you were meeting a girlfriend?'

'I ...' She slunk back in her seat. 'Look, I told you I was meeting a friend so you'd get off my case. And I am - at 5pm. I've got some business first.'

'What business?'

'De Witt Associates. Sponsorship stuff. Bashin's flying over. He's here for two days.'

Trent was losing track. An associate of this. An ambassador for that. She had more roles than phones. And he struggled to read a few revision books. He did knew how many days Bashin had before his fight in Munich, though: three. One of which he'd spend travelling.

'But his camp's already out there,' Trent said.

'It is. I mean, it was -'

'But that's insane, so close to a fight.' The boxer would have tapered down, all the training and sparring done; flying abroad for some poxy promo seemed ludicrous.

She leaned in, the smell of her perfume overpowering his coffee. 'I don't really *know* about boxing.' She drew out the word, like that night at the penthouse. 'It's something we arranged before the fight was agreed. A shoot. For a drinks company.' A black necklace popped out from her fur collar. The same she'd worn with her swimsuit. A saner voice told Trent to push it back.

'That night,' he said. 'You've still never explained why you invited me over.' A gang of road workers walked in. He waited until Mick was out of earshot. 'I could repay the favour. My apartment's close by.'

She fastened her collar. 'As I said, I've work to do.'

'I'll walk with you.'

'No!' She stood. The old guy looked over his paper. A few of the workmen bantering with Mick started to point and laugh. 'And don't attempt to contact me or Lemond again. Or I'll see to it you lose more than your promotion!'

The workmen parted to let her through.

'Hassling you is he, love?'

'Shall we call the police?'

FOURTEEN

Nothing. Not one news report. Even most of the online photos had gone.

He spent the evening channel surfing, waiting for the grainy dawn shot of Stocking and Vondell to appear, but there was little mention of them or Lemond Jackson. Previews of the Munich fight headlined most sports bulletins. A few gossip feeds had rumours of Stocking and the Panamanian being seen together, but nothing of substance, and no images.

It didn't add up.

He woke late the next morning. After a night's wrestling whether to let it go, he'd decided Stocking was a lost cause. He wasn't going to get mugged again. De Witt, however, was a different matter. With the South African it ran deeper. Schalk had followed him to Monaco. You didn't arrange that - or throw around ringside tickets like confetti - if you were whiter than white.

He called Kane and spun some story about needing help with his exam. One o'clock at the Prospect. No, Kane wasn't best pleased about helping a sergeant who'd clearly spent the past few days dicking about instead of revising, but he'd do what he could because he was nice like that.

Trent grabbed his bag. As he walked out he saw his exam notes on the terrace, lying sodden in the rainwater.

Ten minutes later he was on the Docklands Light Railway looping round to Shadwell. The carriage was almost empty. He sat at the front as the train weaved through the gleaming forest of glass and steel. The rise and fall recalled the chopper into Monte Carlo, though without a blue-suited thug in tow. Even so, something was making him restless. It grew worse with each station stop, as if he was being watched from every window above.

FIFTEEN

It wasn't that DCI Frank Kane spent all his time in the Prospect. It was the short work he made of its barrels when he got there.

For decades the pub on the river had been the station local before the move to Whitechapel. It was old school: flagstones on the floor, anchors, wheels and other nautical stuff pinned to the walls. No music. And it had a genuine association with the filth, too: back in the day felons had been transported to Australia from the pier out back. As Kane had told him countless times, legend had it that the post poking from the water at low tide was used for hangings.

Which is where he might end up, if Masterson discovered what he'd been doing.

He was lucky only Kane still drank there.

He cut down onto the cobbles of Wapping Wall. The pub was empty, save for a couple of city guys playing slots and the remnants of a walking tour lunching on the terrace. He found Kane at the back reading a paper.

'You having anything?' He tossed Trent a menu. 'Try the Hunter's Chicken. It's fucking marvellous.'

Trent hadn't eaten properly in days. Beer and Efe's apple cake didn't count. His stomach groaned for a decent meal, but he still didn't fancy it.

'So go on then,' Kane said, after Trent returned from the bar. 'My starter for ten.' He sat back, his fingers spreading over his dart player's paunch.

Trent reached for his rucksack. There was nothing in it but his keys. 'Er … the scenario questions.'

'Yes?'

'They reckon some sections come up more than others. I wondered which ones I should concentrate on.'

'All of 'em.'

Trent stared across to Canary Wharf for inspiration. 'How about older legislation? Like the 1968 Firearms Act?'

'1968?! I was collaring spivs down the King's Road.' Kane raised his pint. 'You should have taken Claire up. Read that crammer she mentioned.'

Trent didn't hear the last bit. On the back page of Kane's paper was a photo of Drey and Bashin in Munich.

'He's here today.'

'You what?'

'Bashin! He's here. Today. In London.'

'No, he ain't. He's sweating his balls off in Munich. For tomorrow night's weigh-in.'

The cheer from the guys at the slot machine turned to a groan.

'I have it on good authority he's not,' Trent said. 'He's meeting Maurice de Witt. In London. Today.'

Kane sank his pint. 'And whose "good authority" might that be, then?'

Trent stared into his bag.

'That bird? Don't tell me you're tapping her up again!' Kane shook his head. 'She's pulling more strings than Gepetto.'

'But don't you think it's strange? A boxer flies all the way from Germany for a promo, only days before his biggest fight?'

'Is that what she said?'

'Promo for some drinks company. Something de Witt arranged.'

'He's his manager, ain't he?'

'Yeah, but -'

'Yeah but it amounts to two sides of nothing. Even if it is true.'

Trent grabbed the paper. The Worlds didn't warrant a mention. He was on the thinnest of ice, with nothing more than Stocking's checking up and his treatment by de Witt's goons to suggest that anything like a conspiracy was possible. But something was going on. He could smell it.

'Give Zimmerman a call,' he said.

'And say what?'

'See if he's got anything on de Witt. Back to the nineties. Earlier, perhaps.'

'He'd have mentioned it by now.'

The walking group was readying to leave. Kane got up.

'Right. I'm off for a fag.'

'Worth a go?' Trent reached into his pocket. 'Buy you another?'

Kane puffed his vein-flecked cheeks.

'Pint. And I'll risk a chaser. Scotch.'

A battered laptop poked from Kane's briefcase. Trent dashed to the bar before firing it up. He'd spent hours overnight searching for dirt on Jackson and Stocking, but had yet to do the same for de Witt.

He tapped away. There were plenty of reports on his East European and Asian fighters going back a decade, though recent coverage was dominated by the de Witt Foundation's charitable work. Nothing that might indict the South African. His nearest brush with the law was as guest of honour at the Police Federation of New Zealand's Christmas lunch.

'Oi - get yer mitts off!' Kane returned. He pretended to

trap Trent's fingers under the screen.

'Shared resources, sir. All part of the efficiency drive.'

'Yeah, well, you be careful.' Kane knocked back his whisky. 'Never know what you'll find on there.' He pulled up a stool. 'What you looking at, anyway?'

'Searching on de Witt. Checking if he's ever sailed close to the wind.'

'He ain't.'

'How do you know?'

Kane pocketed his Regals. 'Our friend Herr Zimmerman just said so.'

Trent sat up. 'You just called him?!'

'Owes us, don't he? I'm all for sharing and caring too, but we ain't gonna be left on the hook for your little jaunt. Not when it was the Germans' idea.'

'But de Witt - what did Zimmerman say?'

'Nothing on him. Told us we're barking up the wrong tree. Or whatever that is in German.' Kane picked up the paper. 'Though it ain't exactly normal, this Bashin flying over, I'll give you that. If your woman's not telling porky-pies, that is.' He skimmed the back page. 'These guys coming in from Asia and the arse-end of Russia. Challenging for belts out of nowhere. You say de Witt's got a few on his books?'

'MMA guys too. Had the dubious pleasure of meeting some.'

The earliest stuff Trent could find was from fifteen years back, intercontinental bouts and prize fighter nights de Witt had promoted in Cape Town and Bloemfontein. After he'd kicked off his Asian operation the action had moved to Kuala Lumpur and Jakarta. The only mildly controversial episode surrounded a disgruntled Kiwi flyweight. The tabloids had kicked up a fuss after the guy, Maori and from a disadvantaged background, had failed to receive his full fight purse. De Witt had eventually settled out of court, with the matter barely warranting a mention after that.

Trent checked the clock. 'Shouldn't you be back at the station?'

Kane started on his beer. He was muttering to himself.

'What is it?'

'Maureece. The way he writes it.'

'And?'

'Pass that here.' Kane typed away. 'Misspellings. He might have used an alternative. Or the journo got it wrong.' He punched in other spellings. The first two brought no results, while the next attempts returned stories they'd already read.

He tapped his pint. With a sigh he typed "Mauritz".

A dozen results came back. Trent leaned in. The articles were from earlier - stretching back to the late nineties. Undercard bouts in regional leisure complexes. De Witt's first media deals.

'Shit the bed!' Kane rocked back. He folded his arms.

'What?'

'*Ernst von Schrader, the disgraced sports doctor, has been handed a two-year suspended sentence from the Central Crown Court. The Austrian national was found guilty of supplying the South African manager Mauritz de Witt and Sheffield boxer Ranji Lane with performance-enhancing substances.* I remember now! Yeah. That scrote of a featherweight from Yorkshire. Good little fighter, mind.'

'And?' Trent said, almost dropping his pint. 'What else does it say?'

'Nothing.'

'That's it?' The *Herald* article was buried in a round-up of other sports. Trent searched for more on Mauritz de Witt and Ranji Lane. The steroid conviction had ended the boxer's comeback after a brief but stellar but career dogged by gambling and recreational drug use. He'd been a tabloid favourite for a couple of years, but little was written about his relationship with de Witt. There'd been a driving conviction that Lane had contested, with witnesses allegedly

94

subjected to intimidation, though the case had been dropped due to lack of evidence. De Witt's name barely made it into print, even alongside Lane's early wins.

'There's nothing!' Trent threw up his arms.

'You what?'

'Nothing on de Witt. Just that one report.'

'That ain't the story.'

'What -'

'Get away -' Kane brushed him aside. He typed. 'I don't call that nothing.' He pulled up a biography of Ernst von Schrader.

'*Born in 1936 in Linz*,' Trent read, '*Von Schrader attended the Borg Liebenau in the city of Graz* ...' He scrolled down. The list of indiscretions was as long as the bar bill at Murdo's leaving do. '... *before providing medical support to leading Eastern Block athletes* ...'

'The name Herman Schiltz ring any bells?'

'Herman the German. Light heavyweight. Got busted for ephedrine?'

'Francis "Driller" Denk. Malachi Som. On von Schrader's books. The lot of 'em.'

The Austrian had used his medical contacts, so the biog had it, to establish a laboratory in London, where he'd revived his work from the East German state doping programmes of the 1980s. Europe-based boxers had used the lab as a stopping-off point for testosterone shots on their way to America, employing von Schrader on an as-and-when basis.

'So what's this von Schrader doing now?' Trent said.

'You might very well ask.' Kane took the laptop. 'Whatever it is, it's different to what he was up to six months ago.' He brought up a news report. After playing the German legal system, von Schrader had finally been extradited to the US, where he'd served eight years for smuggling banned substances. On his release, he'd been hired by a Massachusetts pharmaceutical company, though

95

his employment had been terminated after eighteen months. He'd then moved to the UK.

Six months ago. To London.

'I remember hearing something!' Kane said. 'Yeah, Priestland mentioned it - a few months back.'

'But there'd have been more in the press, surely? I've never heard of the guy.'

Kane sank his pint. 'Knows where the bodies are buried, don't he? Besides, some folk know how to disappear. They've got fixers. Insiders. People who sort such things.'

The Stocking and Vondell photo. Surely that couldn't be suppressed so easily? Not with today's media.

Trent couldn't help whispering, 'You know what I'm thinking ...'

'Yeah. And you've got a nag's chance of being right.'

'If he's here - this von Schrader - he might be sorting out Bashin. With his old mate de Witt.'

Kane grinned. He rummaged in his briefcase.

'The Yanks would have wanted a forwarding address,' Trent went on. 'For von Schrader. It won't be hard find. And we know de Witt always stays in London.'

'Where do you expect him to stay, Margate?' Kane tossed him a tenner. 'Get. I'm off for a snout.'

It was worth a shot. It'd take a day to find out if this supposed promo shoot with Bashin was real, and another to find where von Schrader was hiding. And then there was Vondell. Everything he'd been told so far had come from Jackson and Stocking. He needed to find him. With or without permission.

He came back from the bar. Kane was outside. He was finishing a call.

'Zimmerman again?' Trent said, joining him.

'Er ... no.' Kane pointed over the Thames. 'That post there - you see it? The black stump sticking out the sand? Criminals used to hang there. Murderers, rapists -'

'So what you reckon?'

'About what?'

'This doctor and de Witt. The fact that Alexei Bashin's supposedly on a plane, only two days before the fight of his life, all to flog cans of soda?'

Beyond the gallows a cruiser full of tourists was sailing out from Greenwich pier. Kane puffed on his cigarette. A ball of smoke bowled out over the Thames, shrouding the cruiser in a silver fog.

'We ain't getting involved,' Kane said. 'Even if Bashin is doping, it don't make it criminal.'

'But von Schrader - this Austrian. He's got form.'

'Old bugger probably locked himself away in some basement somewhere. I've heard that's what they do.'

'But if he was bringing in HGH -'

'*If* he were, then we'd have a duty to investigate.'

'There might be a new supply chain. Lemond Jackson top of the list. The rest of de Witt's stable, too.'

Kane stubbed his fag. 'What was that business Claire mentioned? This morning - the girlfriend being papped?'

Trent explained the Hyde Park photo, and how it seemed to vanish within hours

'Pass me that.'

The walking tour had left a copy of the *Times*. Kane flicked to the back pages. Each was dominated by Drey-Bashin.

'Keeps the hype rolling, don't he? For the money-spinner at least.' He flipped to the front. 'Zilch on the Worlds though. You'd think he'd be livid. Promoter should be play merry hell.' He fished in his empty shirt pocket. 'Unless someone don't want their star sprinter anywhere near the press ...'

Trent pulled up a bench. 'And there were those witnesses - in the Lane case. The ones who claimed intimidation.'

'That was years ago. Look, I thought you wanted help with your homework?'

'I did - I mean I do. It's that this could be big. Something's not right. Don't you think so?'

The cruiser chugged eastwards before seeming to stall. It bobbed on the waves for a few seconds, choking out a pall of diesel smoke. Kane watched it turn around. He was more afraid of Masterson's spreadsheets than the magnates, hustlers and bent promoters they went up against. She needed him to land a big one. And this could very well be it.

'See what you can dig up.' Kane groped for his pint. 'And real evidence this time. No more he-says-she-says.'

'Yes, sir.'

'What about leave? Your exam?'

'I'll have time.'

'You hope.'

Trent grabbed his bag. 'I need to find Vondell. If Stocking's supplying him too it might explain why he skipped the toxicology test.'

'Not jealous, are we? You should be careful. You might stumble in while they're at it.' Kane picked up this paper. He turned to the racing tips. 'Though they don't recommend it, do they? Not before a race.' He put on his glasses. 'Saps yer killer instinct ...'

SIXTEEN

Trent shot up the ramp. The black GTI had been a gift from his father after passing basic training, though hell knows where he'd found the money. He'd learned long ago not to ask.

Despite barely making it out of the basement in months, the car looked tired. He'd promised himself something new when he made inspector, though the way he was going he'd be lucky to have a job by Christmas.

The sky above Harbour Quay was stained an angry purple. He sped north towards Stratford. A trio of doormen outside the Welcome Rest had replaced the scrum of photographers. The only fans still around were a group of exhausted Panamanians on the concourse, each wearing a raincoat and holding their national flag. Vondell had left late in the afternoon, they said, to train at the uni track near City airport. They'd tried to get in the previous day, but security had kicked them out. The track had been leased to the Canadian team for the duration of the championships, but Vondell, as the only Panamanian competing, had arranged to share the facility.

The complex was hidden from the main road by tree-lined soccer pitches and a skate park. Floodlights were bearing down on the brick-coloured oval. A prefab reception centre had been set up in front of the entrance. Drifting in and out were guys in double-breasted suits. From the look of it the Canadians had brought their own security, though things were hardly on lock-down.

Trent parked and walked over. Ignoring the staff he ducked the barrier. He'd almost made it to the stands when a hand caught his shoulder.

'Sir, may I ask your business?'

He reached into his pocket.

'Sergeant Trent.' He hesitated for a split-second before flashing his badge. 'Specialist Crime and Operations.'

'Thank you, sir. Are you here to see Darius Vondell?'

Trent nodded.

The guy's teeth outshone the floodlights. Pinned to his jacket was a badge with the maple leaf flag and a motto in English and French.

'Well, I'm sorry sir, but I must ask you to sign in before accessing the athletes' zone. It's kinda protocol.'

They walked back to the portakabin. A whole load of paparazzi had come by after Vondell had been released on police bail, the guard said, somewhat excitedly. Other law enforcement officers had also passed by after the hotel incident. They'd wanted to speak with the sprinter's management team, only to be told he didn't have one.

'Can you believe that!' The guard pointed to where Trent should sign. 'I imagine you're here about his bail conditions. You know you can't condone what he did n'all, but you gotta feel sorry for him, don't you think so? Facing all those accusations, all the press. Seems no-one was looking out for him.'

Trent was itching to get away. 'Has anyone else come by here today? A woman perhaps?'

'Just fans. Some even claiming to be his "entourage", but we get all kinds of wackos in this job, you know.' He raised his arm. For a moment Trent thought he was going to salute. 'Thank you for your understanding, officer.' He took Trent's hand. 'And sir, let me again apologise. As a fellow law enforcement professional you'll understand ...'

Around a dozen athletes were still out in the twilight. A group of runners were doing circuits around the pot-holed oval, each taking turns to set the pace. To the far side, a solitary pole-vaulter was checking his run-up.

Trent eventually found Vondell, lurking in the shadow of the tatty south stand. He was wearing black tights and stripped to the waist. Laughing and joking with him were a couple of women, long-jumpers it seemed.

Trent leaned on a steeplechase barrier. He watched Vondell burst into 50m sprints, his squat figure a powerhouse of muscle and sinew. Each run was followed by a thirty-second recovery walk, though every few reps he'd break off to check his phone or speak with the women, who seemed far more interested in him than their own training.

The seats were empty, save for a coach barking at the runners. Vondell had no one. From what Trent understood he did have a long-term trainer, a Jamaican former 400m man who'd come out of retirement to help him with his speed endurance, though the relationship was rocky and they rarely travelled together. His band of 'wackos', as the security guy called them, seemed to have been ditched in the wake of the hotel débacle. The press might not paint Vondell as the sharpest pin in the box, but at least he had the sense to knuckle down before the biggest race of his life.

Or so it seemed.

Vondell put on his headphones. He started out on what looked like warm-down laps. Trent waited until he passed by on the bend.

'No management,' Trent called out loudly. 'No trainer. Must be difficult, doing all this alone.'

Vondell shot him a look, but didn't break stride.

'Risky strategy. Even for the world's fastest.'

The Panamanian stopped. Front-on he was even wider than on TV, his torso like a sculpted side of beef. At the peak of each mountainous shoulder was a deltoid the size of a cannonball, a snake stretching down his right arm. In the tattoo department, at least, he had Jackson beat.

'Who the fuck are you? Where's the camera?' Vondell ran over. 'Your camera!' He stuck a hand in Trent's face. 'Where is it?'

'Hey!' Trent raised his arms. 'You don't need to do this.' He flashed his ID.

'Do what?' Vondell stepped back. 'Uh-uh. That lawyer they got me: you speak to her. I've said enough.'

'It's not about the hotel.'

'Then get the fuck away from me.' Vondell pulled on his headphones.

'You know Gabrielle Stocking?'

'The hell you asking me for?'

'I've seen the photo.'

'What photo?'

'This morning. In Hyde Park.'

Vondell removed his cans. 'I don't know nothing about no park.'

Trent rounded the barrier. He knew about the affair, he said. How long it had been going on. Lemond Jackson had told him everything.

A laugh from one of the long jumpers echoed down the stand. Vondell rubbed his eyes.

'Yeah, well. Whatever. The loser got played. Took his record. Nailed his girl. Suppose the dupe cooked-up some other shit on me. That's why he sent you, right?'

This guy talked as fast as he ran. Trent wriggled through the barrier and out onto the track.

'So long, officer. I gotta train.'

'Just a few questions -'

'What the fuck's it to do with you?' Vondell squared up, his pecs like plates of gunmetal. 'Go find her if there's a problem.'

Trent had one. But he'd promised to let it go. Blurt it here and he'd have an even bigger one; even Vondell's fists had muscles.

'Look.' He rested on a hurdle stack. 'I could take you down the station, or we could have a sensible little chat right here. Off the record. Just you and me.' Mist was falling on the outfield. Above them the floodlights flared white and buzzed with insects. 'Ten minutes?'

'You got five.' Vondell picked up his vest. He stormed back towards the long jump pit.

'Must have been hard. Taking the press rap.' Trent said, jogging to keep up. 'The Berlin official ... all that crap you took -'

'Say what?'

'You bought it. Even after the women official dropped her complaint, the press all assumed you started it.'

Vondell stopped. He stabbed a finger in Trent's chest. 'Jackson ... the way he walks around ... like he's the man -'

'Three Olympic golds. He is the man.'

Vondell smiled. He shook his head and walked on.

'On the warm-up track,' Trent said, 'there's protocol, isn't there? About respecting someone's practice space?'

Vondell's holdall lay in the shot-putt circle. He pulled out his Gatorade.

'I ran in his lane. So what? Ain't like I smoked the bitch. Though after what they did to me,' he threw down his bottle, 'they sure would've deserved it.'

'Who's "they"? The person who spiked your drink?'

Vondell zipped his bag. He stormed back to the jumpers. The accusation seemed real, even if he'd not chosen to pursue it. And it was still bothering him far more than whatever was going on between him, Jackson and Stocking. He couldn't care less what the media knew or didn't know about their relationships. That was obvious. It was the same attitude that had helped the press cement his bad-boy status. He spoke, they listened. But that didn't mean they liked him.

'Look man, I know my body. The way I felt before Berlin - how quickly it came on - hell, I thought I was dying out there.' Vondell picked up his tracksuit.

'But you didn't follow up your accusation.'

'I never accused nobody. Not by name.'

'You could have had a toxicology test.'

The jumpers were leaving. As the taller woman pulled on her tights Vondell gently tipped her over, sending her compatriot into fits of laughter. He whispered in her ear.

'Don't do hospitals,' Vondell said, pulling on his jersey. 'Had enough of that shit as a kid.'

His adoptive parents had found him in an orphanage in callipers, Trent had learned. Corrective surgery had straightened his legs, but he'd only started sprinting in high school.

'Any more?' Vondell eyed-up the women. "Cos this pair are late for their bedtimes.' He dangled some BMW keys.

Trent slapped a mosquito on his arm. If the Panamanian had been sabotaged in Berlin, the evidence was long gone. Whatever might be going on with Jackson and de Witt was another story. Though one with the same female character.

Stocking.

'Does the name Ernst von Schrader mean anything to you?' Trent said.

'No.'

Tyres squealed in the parking lot. 'Gabby never mention him?'

'Nope.'

Trent explained the Austrian's dealings with de Witt.

Vondell raised an eyebrow. 'And this quack's supplying de Witt now?'

'Er ... no. Well, we don't -'

'So you're telling me, that Maureece de Witt, daddy of the golden child Lemond Jackson, is working with a convicted doper?' Vondell shook his head, incredulously. 'Damn, they gotta hear this!'

He pulled out his phone. Trent tried to swipe it.

'Who?'

Vondell swatted him away. 'The press. All this shit on me … well, it's time for that dude to take the heat.'

'You can't! I mean, we're still investigating -'

'Then why you telling me?' Trent felt his hole deepening. He shouldn't have mentioned it. 'Look, I can help you.'

Someone shouted. Over by the security hut one of the guards was arguing with another man – one of the athletes, it seemed.

'Help me? With what?'

'Berlin.' Trent said, panicking. 'Finding out what really happened.'

Vondell called to the jumpers. 'Yeah, well, that's gonna have to wait. 'Cos I've got business.'

Trent glanced at the waiting women.

'No man!' Vondell said, uncharacteristically shocked. 'I got me a world title to win!'

'You're not to mention any of this,' Trent stuttered. 'Not to the media. Not until I've -'

'You said you'd help me out. Sounds like we got a deal?'

Trent fumbled for a pen. His palms were sweating. 'Okay. What's your number?'

Vondell scribbled it down. It was the same one Kane had confirmed in Monaco.

'You didn't say - you and Stocking - so it's over now?'

'We're done here, man.'

'I can see the attraction. Model. Goodwill ambassador. She's even writing a novel, I hear.'

Vondell threw back his head. 'Ha-ha! That's right. What do they say? "Multi-talented".' He clapped Trent's shoulder.

105

'But I only went there for one thing, right?'

'Went there? So it is over?'

'Darius -' One of the jumpers pointed across the outfield. The man who'd been arguing with security was running over.

Vondell's glint disappeared. 'We're done.'

Trent raised his hands in mock-submission. He started back around the track. The skinny guy rushing over the outfield was also wearing tights and had his hood pulled up. It was only when he removed it that Trent saw it was Jad Gaines. Steam puffed sharply from his mouth. He started gesticulating, his voice urgent.

Half of the floodlights had been turned off. Trent slipped into the shadows of the outfield. He pretended to tie his shoelace as the sprinters spoke. They had to go, Gaines seemed to be saying. Vondell was resisting, pointing back at the confused jumpers. Gaines tried to drag him away, only to draw a string of expletives from the Panamanian.

The Canadian jumpers gave up and started back down the straight. Trent dodged into the stand. Why the hell would Jackson's friend and team mate be crashing the training facility of their biggest rival, just days before their heats?

Gaines waited for the jumpers to enter the locker room. He marched back across the grass, Vondell in tow. The guard who'd challenged Trent said something, only to be pushed aside as the pair vaulted the safety barrier and disappeared into the parking lot.

SEVENTEEN

Trent passed through security to see a midnight blue Z4 streak out by the skate park. He jumped into his car and followed behind, keeping a minibus of Canadians between him and Vondell.

The sprinters accelerated once past the waste ground. They were heading back to Vondell's hotel, it seemed. Whatever was troubling Gaines, it was important enough for Vondell to ditch his female fan club. Trent had planned to spend the evening following up on von Schrader's whereabouts, but something was stirring here. He knew Jackson and Gaines were close after seeing them in Berlin, and the American had confirmed they were training together only that morning. But Gaines and Vondell? If the former was a confidant of Jackson, surely that ruled out friendship with the Panamanian?

Ad banners for the championships hung from every street light in Canning Town. All featured Jackson crossing a finish line, his arm raised. By his shoulder was a smaller image of Vondell, his strained features in stark contrast to Jackson's joyous face of victory.

The lights turned red. Trent made out silhouettes of the

two men in the BMW. They were talking animatedly. He waited for them to pull off again, moving to their blind spot fifty feet behind. At East India Dock the BMW swung over onto the A12. Three minutes later the white-lit crown of the stadium emerged between the broken landscape of storage units and graffiti-daubed warehouses.

At the next junction, Vondell indicated left. Trent slowed, tracking him as he doubled back under the carriageway. Lights stopped them under the flyover. Trent inched forward. As the signal turned amber, a tombstone grey Vectra undercut him, slotting itself in behind Vondell.

The light went green. The Vectra revved massively, its nose up the Z4's rear. The signal changed. Vondell slammed forward, only to stall. He accelerated again. The Vectra tried to go around him, but was driven wide by a split pedestrian crossing. Swerving to avoid an oncoming car, it lurched back towards Vondell's BMW.

An unmarked interceptor, Trent thought? No, they'd have the siren blaring by now.

Vondell was being followed.

The main entrance to Stadium Park was to their left. Vondell veered towards it as the Vectra drew level. They slowed. Vondell indicated to turn, bringing the Vectra closer, only to lurch away at the last second. He flew back up the ramp. Under a blanket of smoke he raced past the media centre. Seconds later he swung into the A12 traffic and headed back towards Docklands.

Trent scrambled for his phone. Whatever plans Gaines had for the evening, someone had other ideas.

'Claire, it's Trent!' he yelled back at her voicemail. 'One of the American sprinters - Jad Gaines. Golf-Alpha-Indigo-November-Echo-Sierra. Something's going on between him and Darius Vondell. I want to know how far they go back - when they first competed -'

He dropped the phone. As they curved down towards the river, the Vectra swung into the fast line, attempting to pass Vondell again. The BMW pulled out, forcing its pursuer closer to the central reservation. Trent made to move into the middle lane, only to be blocked by a speeding truck.

A sign flashed up: a mile to the Blackwall tunnel. He couldn't lose them. Once out the other side they'd be away into Kent.

'Damn it!' He smashed his fist on the wheel. A line of traffic was backing up at the next lights, with no sign of Vondell or the Vectra. Skeletons of new high rises clawed skyward on both sides of the road, as if desperate to escape the smog.

Trent revved behind a van. On green he screeched around. Twenty seconds later the road narrowed as the tunnel approached. He cut-up an idling 4x4, then weaved between more cars as the road dived towards the river.

Vondell's number. He ripped it from his pocket. If he didn't answer, maybe Gaines would.

'*No man, wait -*'

'*I told you, they're behind -*'

More than one conversation was taking place. Gaines was speaking. On another call, it seemed.

'Vondell! It's Sergeant Trent - we spoke - '

He saw them. A hundred yards ahead, a low-loader had drawn out in front, barring their entry to the tunnel. Trent put his foot down. Vondell was jinking left and right, the Z4 now missing a brake light. Below it his bumper appeared to have been struck, its left side flapping open like a fish tail.

'Darius!' Trent shouted. 'Just tell me -'

The tunnel cut him off. They plunged into the semi-darkness, diving deep under the Thames. Ignoring the speed restriction, the Vectra got a jump on Vondell and flew by the low loader. Its brake lights flared as it tried to block the BMW, only for Vondell to squeeze through on the inside.

109

Trent accelerated. To his left, the filthy lights along the pedestrian walkway passed in a blur. He caught them around the bend and tried for a better sight of Vondell's damage, only for the Vectra to swing out and block his view. With no attempt to pass this time it slammed sidewards, colliding with the rear of the BMW and making it hop like a frightened rabbit.

The crunch cut through the engine drone. Undeterred, Vondell sped on. An orange signal above indicated a closing lane. Vondell swung over and hugged the walkway wall. As they emerged into the open air, Trent realised his phone was ringing.

'Claire!'

'You're driving - what's -'

Bollards signalled the lane's imminent closure. Ignoring them, the Vectra stayed its course, ploughing several aside. Trent swerved, only to drop his phone again. Realising they were about to run out of lane, the Vectra's driver scythed inwards, striking Vondell on the nearside wing. The Z4 shivered, as if jolted by a cattle prod, before spinning and colliding with the kerb. All four wheels left the ground. With a groan it flipped. Trent shot out from behind the Vectra in time to see the BMW land on its roof. It rolled twice over some waste ground before coming to rest in the shadow of a gas holder.

Trent slammed on his brakes. Ahead of him, the Vectra pulled into the scrub and started to crawl across the broken concrete. A barrier and kiosk marked what looked like a forgotten truck stop. Unable to drive on, a figure leapt from the passenger seat and ran towards the smoking wreck. In his hand was a weapon, a baseball bat or cosh.

Trent mounted the kerb. He grabbed a torch from the glove box and ditched the car. The place stank. Ringing the wrecked BMW were rusting refrigerators, mattresses and other crap, as if they'd landed at some nightmare campsite.

'Police! Put it down!'

The figure was wearing a black bomber jacket, a beanie pulled low of his brow. The man hesitated by Vondell's mangled car, as if ready to drop whatever he was carrying, only to change his mind.

Trent yelled again. The assailant dodged behind a mound of dead fridges and sprinted back towards the Vectra. Trent clambered over a twisted bed frame, but the man was already in his car. With a screech the Vectra shot backwards, showering Trent in grit, before spinning and roaring away across the rubble. A distant siren fluttered on the wind as it hurtled into the distance, fleeing south on the half-empty carriageway.

Trent covered his mouth. Black smoke pumped from Vondell's tyres. The impact had crushed the roof, the back window popped open like a tin can.

Someone moved inside. Trent stepped over the broken glass, only to tread on something hard. It was a phone - a burner, its screen cracked but still working.

He stuffed it in his jacket and threw aside the car's bumper. He ran his light along the fender. The driver's door was ajar. Beneath it, a glut of oil had seeped out and was blackening the concrete.

He kicked open the door, only to recoil in horror. A tattooed wrist hung down. It was not oil dripping from the car, he realised, but blood.

And the dead man at the wheel was not Darius Vondell.

It was Jad Gaines.

EIGHTEEN

'So you're not on the Murder Investigation Team?'

Trent explained. Or tried to. He was sick of this - justifying his own unit - especially now their involvement was legit. Sort of.

The officer at the Royal London's entrance spoke with a colleague. Behind them a detachment from the investigation team was being harangued by some older guys in tracksuits - a delegation from the US team, by the looks of it. The place stank of old blankets and disinfectant. Like all hospitals. Visitors and porters pushing patients filled the packed lobby. He'd seen no Vondell supporters that morning, but there was little room for their flags and banners here.

Kane was by a vending machine eating a cheese roll. Trent looked for Claire. He'd expected her there, too.

'Where's the patient?'

Kane wiped his mouth. 'Gone.'

'What?'

'Discharged himself. Before I arrived.'

'You're kidding?!' Trent spun around. 'I thought he had head injuries?!'

'Cuts. Bit of bruising. Brain scan was clear. Least he never trashed the place.'

Vondell had spent the night under armed guard in a private room. Besides the superficial wound to his forehead, some flying glass had cut his arm, though not badly enough for stitches. He'd had no visitors and made no calls. The docs had wanted him in for another night but Vondell, his temper flaring, had insisted on leaving that morning.

Trent sat. The US delegation were complaining about a lack of information. Others were weeping, heads in hands. Gaines' body had been brought there with the autopsy planned for the day after the 100m final, though there was little doubt in Trent's mind that he'd been killed by a head strike to the steering column.

Gaines and Lemond Jackson had been close. There was enough in what he'd been piecing together about de Witt and the Austrian doctor to suspect anyone connected with the South African's stable, even if he hadn't actually been Gaines' manager.

'Who took your statement?' Kane said.

The station was ten minutes away. Trent had given it there.

'New guy. Haven't seen him before.'

'Who's the DCI?'

'Rabbatts.'

Kane pulled a face. 'Great. Just what we need. A fast-tracker who jumps in with both feet. Masterson don't rate him either.'

Trent nodded at the murder squad. 'You spoken to them?'

The team had been there all night, Kane explained, finally interviewing Vondell in the early hours after his scan. He'd claimed in his statement that Gaines had sped over after hearing someone was out to do Vondell harm, and that he'd needed to tell him in person. Gaines' reluctance to name the source had led to an argument in the car. Then

113

they'd seen the Vectra.

'So how come Gaines was driving?' Trent said.

'Pissed off about the banger his team had rented. Fancied a razz in the Z4. Simple as that.'

'And they were heading back to Vondell's hotel?'

'He says not. Just driving around, he reckons, having a chit-chat. Gaines didn't want anyone else to hear.'

Or see them together, Trent thought. 'So Gaines had to come back for his rental?'

'Apparently.' Kane nodded at the murder squad. 'Took that lot another hour to prise Bad Boy's plans out of him. For the rest of the night, I mean.'

'Which were?'

Kane eased himself from the plastic chair. 'Seeing Jackson's missus again. Some bar in the mall, apparently. The one near to his hotel. To clear the air.'

'What time?'

'Late-ish. 10pm. He never said nothing?'

Trent shook his head. The BMW had crashed around 8.30pm. Still long enough to drop Gaines back for his car and return to the mall. It was plausible. Though Vondell hadn't mentioned it at the track. He might well be lying, given his apparent plans for the women long jumpers - and his reputation in general.

Kane sniffed. He reached for his coat. 'You spoken to Rabbatts?'

'No. Some junior took the statement. That was it. Said they'd call if they needed more.'

The guys from the investigation team were pointing over. One of the US delegation, an ex-athlete judging by his build, was nodding at Trent.

'Come on.' Kane grabbed his cuff. 'I need a smoke.'

They slipped out of a side door. By the wall was a huge yellow trash can labelled 'sharps'.

'Investigation team want us to take a back seat,' Kane said, lighting up. 'It's their baby now. By the sounds of it

Rabbatts hasn't spoken to Masterson, but it won't be long.'

'But they can't, I mean, I'm the only witness.'

'Conflict of interest, ain't it? Besides, it's a murder inquiry now.'

Trent remembered his promise to Vondell. But that was before Gaines had been killed.

'Someone's after Vondell. Surely, after Berlin -'

'His dicky tummy? You said there was nothing in it.'

'So what are Rabbatt's team's thinking about motive?'

Kane smirked. He flicked his stub away. 'Robbery.'

'You what?'

'Opportunists. Saw the flash car and fancied it.'

'But there were two of them in there! The Vectra had tinted windows. I told them that. There's no way this was a robbery!'

Kane shrugged.

'What about the burner they dropped?'

'Still in forensics.' Kane's phone buzzed. 'Though lucky we're not waiting on them for everything.' He held up a message. It was from Claire. 'The Vectra. Bought at auction under alias last week. Ran the plate through the automated reader. Spotted around 8.40pm last night. They lost it around Dartford.'

Trent grinned. Kane's couldn't even spell protocol. He got things done instead. And neither was Masterson above turning the odd blind eye to his antics. Not when it suited her.

Trent revealed what Claire had dug up on Vondell and Gaines. Turns out they'd been freshmen together at Michigan State, though once Vondell had dropped out they'd not raced each other until two years later. Gaines appeared to have been a late-developer, completing his studies before belatedly making the US team. He was the polar opposite to Vondell, a quiet teetotaller from a track and field family.

The perfect training mate on the edge of Jackson's

spotlight. Given Vondell's reputation as a loner, it was even harder to see how the pair might be close.

'Did Gaines say anything to Vondell about Jackson?' Trent said. 'I mean, he could have been spying on him - slipping him secrets - Jackson's training regime, his diet and stuff. And if this von Schrader ...'

'Whoa -' Kane lit another fag. 'Hold your horses. Gaines never said nothing about Jackson. Not according to Bad Boy's statement.' He fished out a crumpled note.

'What's that?'

'Read.'

It was Jackson's press release. The champion expressed his condolences to the family and friends of Gaines, who had been more like a brother than a training partner. The whole US team were heartbroken, and would find it hard to come to terms with the loss of a beloved friend and competitor. Anyone who has lost someone close would question whether it was right to carry on at such a time. But what Gaines would have wanted most would be for the US team to realise the dreams they'd all trained so hard for. It was in this spirit that Jackson would compete in London. He would run in Gaines' memory, doing everything in his power to win gold for his country.

Trent flipped the paper. *Lemond Jackson Management.* No mention of de Witt by name.

'So I guess Jackson will have a free run in the final. Vondell can't race with his arm in a sling.'

'It ain't in a sling.'

Kane turned. Outside the police cordon a group of men with cameras were exiting a van.

'Anyway, he's probably heading back to the States right now.'

'We thought that last time.'

The van guys were from the press. They jostled at the entrance trying to get in, while a few feet away some women from the delegation, family members for all Trent knew, were hugging in tears.

There was no way this was a robbery, however violent. Someone was out for Vondell or Gaines. Stocking wasn't going to be giving answers any time soon, and if she wasn't returning his calls she sure as hell wouldn't be volunteering for questioning.

Doping. It had to be in there somewhere. It usually was. And it wouldn't take him long to find out who Bashin's drinks sponsor was in the UK.

Or learn where this needle merchant von Schrader was living now.

Kane's phone rang. 'It's Her Ladyship.'

'What you gonna say?'

'What I've told you. Make sure Rabbatts' team don't end up like muppets playing Cluedo.'

The American who'd spied Trent was coming over. He'd want Trent's account of the crash, but he'd have to wait for the coroner's report, like everybody else.

'I'm going to follow up on this Bashin promo,' Trent said. 'And find the Austrian doc.'

Kane stuck up a thumb. Before Trent could say more he was giving Masterson an earful.

Trent was pushing his way through the media when he saw the photographer in the Arsenal cap from the Verdana Spa. The guy's mouth fell open, his eyes flitting to where Trent's dodgy lanyard had hung. Before he could spy his police ID, Trent jogged out through the parking lot and away into the Whitechapel traffic.

He weaved between the market stalls. At the bottom of Brick Lane he slipped on something. He peeled a sodden piece of cardboard from his ankle. The blue, white and red had been discoloured by rotten chicken boxes, but it was still just about recognisable as a Panamanian flag, greasy and torn amongst the bones.

NINETEEN

'Damn it, come on!'

Trent punched the horn. Ten minutes he'd been there. He'd left London after the morning rush hour, only to be caught in lane closures around the stadium. All the traffic east looked choked.

Eight hours to go. Jackson's heat, the first, was scheduled for 8.45pm. A spokesman had confirmed Vondell's entry in Heat 4, though the papers had all but dismissed his chances of appearing. Trent had tried calling him again, to no avail.

That wasn't the only thing pissing him off. After leaving Kane, he'd spent the rest of the morning trying to locate Bashin. A call to de Witt's Zurich office had met with a stream of obscenities. Realising he wasn't going to get any help there, he'd rang around the London media agencies. An intern had finally blabbed: Bashin had been booked for a session in Clerkenwell that afternoon, minutes from Mick's café. Trent had spooked her with talk of a police investigation and she'd coughed up right away: the Belarusian had been photographed as part of a drinks promotion. The shoot had barely lasted an hour, with the fighter whisked off at the end by a statuesque blonde.

The whole thing had escaped the press. Again. If de Witt was willing to risk Bashin's preparation for some poxy sponsorship, it didn't say much for his fight chances. Or the size of his purse.

Trent crawled forward. The lights turned red again. He swiped down his phone, seeing the number of unanswered calls he'd made to Stocking. He felt embarrassed. The murder squad would be doing a trace. He'd explained his dealings with her - well, some of it, at least - but they'd find out pretty sharpish that he'd been buzzing her more than was acceptable.

Harassment, she'd called it. And knowing her she'd have de Witt's best lawyers ready-primed.

Inspector Trent. It all seemed a long, long way off.

A message popped up:

The Retreat
Hopkins Lane
Eastwold

'Bingo.'

Ernst von Schrader's address.

He'd found enough to suggest the Austrian had settled in Suffolk, but he wasn't on any of the usual lists. Claire had come good - again. If Masterson hadn't taken against her she'd be making inspector before him.

Once deeper into Suffolk the road cleared. He put his foot down past the pretty villages of Dedham Vale. The area had been a favourite for weekend visits as a child, but all those memories were lost behind the black cloud that would forever haunt the fields.

For it was here, on the road outside his home town, where his mother had lost her life.

No longer did he associate the area with fishing trips and train rides, where even his father had occasionally turned up to buy him an ice cream. Even after all these years, the sight of a dark blue van had him checking the

119

licence plate, uselessly, like there was something he could still do. They'd been no traffic cameras, then. No witnesses with mobile phones. And he knew, better than most, that finding a hit-and-runner ten years on was as likely as Kane going sober.

He remembered his father's call, but little after that. He'd shut out the pain. For a year he'd thought of dropping out of uni, leaving London and returning to Colchester. But there was nothing for him here. His father soon met someone else. A degree in management and psychology wasn't going to bring her back, but it was better than rotting away in some dead-end job back home.

In time he'd learned to draw on his mother's memory as a source of inspiration. But the violent reality of what happened would never leave him. It had been there that day, in Mick's, when he'd signed the papers, applying for the Force.

It was always there.

TWENTY

Eastwold was picture-postcard pretty, a former fishing port turned exclusive seaside retreat for Londoners. Out of season, however, it was a ghost town of second homes, deserted save for vans delivering posh cheese.

If an ageing criminal wanted somewhere to disappear to, this might very well be the place.

He parked near the pier. The map showed Hopkins Lane at the far end of the promenade, down towards some wetland meadows. A strip of fisherman's cottages lined the beachhead. Walking the cobbles he remembered the pictures he'd seen of the Austrian. The few reports he'd found on the Ranji Lane case had shown archive snaps of the white-coated doctor working with Eastern Block athletes. Even without hard evidence the images were damning, and it wasn't hard to see why the Sheffield boxer had quickly slipped from local hero into notoriety. Von Schrader's appearance had been a gift to the British press: lean, balding, with glasses like picture frames, he came straight out of Communist Bad Guy casting. It made the trial's lack of press coverage even more suspicious.

The Retreat. He expected some grand entrance tucked

away down a private road. Doubling back he checked the names and numbers of the cottages. He'd walked a good half mile down the coast, but was sure he hadn't missed it. Eventually the cobbles petered out into grassland. Down the side of the last cottage, behind a crumbled outbuilding and some rusting farm machinery, lay a ramshackle barn. The ground floor windows were all but hidden by an overgrown hedge running around the lawn, but there was no doubt it was inhabited. An ancient Morris Minor, its front wheel punctured, lay rusting outside.

He walked down a rough track. A sign stuck out of the mud. The wooden post had all but disintegrated, but he could just make out the words above.

The Retreat.

Someone was working out front. Trent peered through the hedge. An elderly man in a safari shirt was holding a flower basket. The gardener, he guessed.

'Hello there!' The figure stuck up his nose, like a rare butterfly had passed.

He went back to his pruning.

Trent rattled the gate. 'Hi, I'm looking for Doctor von Schrader. Does he live here?'

The gardener looked over. He crouched as if to put down his basket and secateurs, only to decide against it.

'Who is asking?'

Trent's hand slipped from the latch. The face was thinner and the glasses were gone. He was also shorter than in the photos. But the Austrian accent cut the haze like a knife.

'Doctor von Schrader? I'm Detective Sergeant Trent. From the Metropolitan Police. Specialist Crimes and Operations.'

The upper floor of the barn was unpainted and shuttered, as if a conversion had run out of money. To one side of a weedy path was a stagnant pond. Thermometers poked out through a brown film of water. It looked like a punctured mattress.

Von Schrader shuffled back towards his door.

'Please go. I have nothing more to say.'

A pile of leaking pesticide tins blocked the gate. Trent clambered over. The garden smelt of wet cinders. There was a vague tang of ammonia.

'I just want to ask you a few questions, sir.' Trent waved his badge.

'The government's signed my protection agreement. There is nothing more to discuss.'

Protection agreement? This was news to Trent. 'No, sir, it's about -'

'Go now. I have nothing more -'

'It's about Maureece de Witt.'

The doctor's hand sprang from the door handle, as if it were white hot. With heavy, nasal breaths he turned. A couple of days' beard growth sprouted from his chin. It gave his face an impish energy, despite his stoop.

'What of him?'

'Ranji Lane. The doping case. I want to know more about de Witt's involvement.'

Von Schrader paused. He looked skywards. 'Ah yes! A beautiful boy, no? So sad, what happened.' His colour changed, as if a ghost had departed. 'Who is it you say you work for?'

Trent ran through his unit's remit. He sketched out de Witt's foray into track and field, but held back on his suspicions.

The Austrian handed him his secateurs. 'The camellia. By my friend David over there. It blocks my view.'

'David?'

Von Schrader nodded towards the hedge. A life-size statue of a naked man faced the foliage.

'I shall make tea.'

He disappeared inside. Trent set about the bush, keeping an eye on the doctor in his kitchen. It was hard to see how this little guy had penetrated the boxing world, let alone masterminded the enhanced performance of an entire generation of East German athletes. But if there's one thing he'd learned about sports crime, it was that there was always brains behind the bluster. You just followed the money.

The doctor returned, sloshing tea over a tray. He picked his way across the lawn.

'A view to cherish, no?'

Trent gazed through the hole he'd cut. A couple of container ships sat motionless on the horizon. The last of the morning mist was burning off the Thames estuary, exposing a spit of dune to the south.

Von Schrader put down the drinks. 'There, you see, no?' Dotted across the sandbanks, a couple of miles out to sea, were a series of grey bunkers, their pillared walls topped with thick concrete roofs. 'For testing nuclear trigger devices. They used the area for weapons development after the war. All very secret, of course. They look like something from ancient Rome, no?'

Trent huffed. He dreaded to think what else the Austrian might once have worked on, back in the day.

'You've not been here long,' Trent said, surveying the garden. 'Seems a lonely place for someone well travelled.'

'I'm retired, sergeant. You did say sergeant?'

Trent did. He didn't need reminding.

'Yes, well. I'm happy here. The nearest train station's thirty minutes west.'

Trent glanced at the written-off car.

'No, no. No longer can I drive.' Von Schrader felt his lower back. 'What they did ... I mean, because of my time in prison.' He handed Trent a mug. 'It suits me very well. Just me, my experiments and papers.' He raised his tea, as if toasting his new life.

'So you're no longer involved in any ... sporting work?'

'You asked me about the boxer. I'm giving you my time. Now give me your questions.'

For the first time Trent met von Schrader's eyes. Black dots ringed with pale green, the colour of antifreeze. Lane had approached him via an intermediary, he said, with de Witt apparently only learning of the boxer's drug taking much later on. At his trial, Lane had protected the South African, refusing to admit he knew anything.

'So who dobbed Lane in?'

'Dobbed?'

'Grassed. Testified.'

'Ah. The intermediary. A man I trusted. This person wasted no time in naming me too.' Von Schrader sipped his tea. 'Someone must have made him, how do they say, "an offer he couldn't refuse".'

'De Witt.'

The doctor tapped mugs. 'Clever boy. I see now why you're a policeman.'

Trent cast his dregs across the lawn. And the South African got away scot-free as part of the deal, the whole episode barely troubling the press, no doubt.

'What happened to him, this intermediary?'

Von Schrader picked up the secateurs. He thrust an arm into the camellia. 'No one has seen or heard from him since.'

'But you went to jail! Your career here was finished. Wasn't de Witt to blame?'

A small jug lay on the drinks tray. The doctor picked it up. 'Tell me, Sergeant Trent, do you drink pasteurised milk?'

'Er ... I buy it from the supermarket.'

'Then you do. So you are comfortable in the manipulation of nature to enhance your health - your physical performance, one might say?'

Trent frowned. Was he meant to answer?

'And when you were younger, a teenager, perhaps, you were inoculated against tuberculosis?'

Trent nodded. He saw where this was heading.

125

Von Schrader raised both arms to the sea, as if it might part on his command. 'Ever since we have realised something of our biology we have sought to make improvements, however small, to compete within our race! That is in itself human, no?'

No, *Herr* Doctor. Stretch it as far as you like, but it's not enough to justify a lifetime's cheating.

'You didn't answer my question,' Trent said. 'You went down. De Witt saw to it.'

The sun found its way through the hole in the bush. Von Schrader grabbed more branches and began to hack away.

'That is the thing, you know, about prison. Many things you learn - about criminals, the way they operate.' Trent offered to help but was waved away. 'The bloated fool still owes me Deutschmarks. More than a million, to be precise.' He wiped his forehead. 'You say your unit works independently, away from other police teams, yes?'

'Mostly.'

The Austrian unbuttoned his shirt. He sat wearily by his statue. 'Your colleagues who come here. The ones who also wear no uniform. They shall not know what I am going to tell you, yes?'

'I promise.' Trent zipped his mouth. He had no idea what this secret arrangement was. Something told him it should stay that way.

Pawtuckett Correctional Institution was a low-to-medium security facility housing mostly white-collar inmates, von Schrader explained. Many were perpetrators of organised crimes such as banking fraud and insurance scams. One group would sit for hours playing cards in the canteen. Eventually he'd befriended them by teaching them bridge. Each man had been convicted of gambling crimes, he'd discovered - match fixing, mostly.

He gave a wistful look, as if he'd glimpsed another rare butterfly.

'They would speak of these overlords. Underworld figures. Many in the Far East, Central America, directing huge betting syndicates, amongst other things. Mythical figures, almost.' He laughed and shook his head. 'They were terrified, beneath all the bravado, really they were! But you should have heard them. They spoke with such awe!'

'And?'

'One day the name Maureece de Witt was mentioned. Naturally, I did not reveal my own acquaintance - you learn to be careful, no? Well, the talk was that he had become, how do you say, "under the thumb" ...'

'Of?'

The Austrian swallowed, his throat swelling like a bullfrog's.

'Of El Castillo.'

'Who?' The name meant nothing.

'Once before I had heard of this person, back in the seventies. No more after that. Not until that day in the jail. If this Castillo did exist I imagined he'd died many years ago.'

'What did you know then? And what's this Castillo up to now?'

Von Schrader stood. He rubbed his back again. 'There's not much these networks aren't involved in, from what I understand.'

Trent blocked his path. 'Where does Castillo operate from?'

'Manila. Possibly. My bridge partners went only on hearsay, you understand. Of course they might have been lying. They were criminals, after all.'

'So he's Filipino?'

'Filipino. Spanish. Could be Egyptian for all anyone knows.'

For the first time Trent felt irritated. The doctor was the kind to withhold evidence simply because he could. Though his wrist was trembling. Mentioning this Castillo had clearly touched a nerve.

'Castillo - does he -'

'Maureece de Witt,' von Schrader said, raising his voice, 'had dealings with him as recently as one year ago! That is all that is deducible from my story. I have nothing more.' He whipped the tea towel from the statue. 'Take some advice, *mein Junge*: when dealing with forces you do not understand, it is not wise to gossip with strangers. And we do not know each other, Sergeant Trent, despite your promise earlier.' He ran his fingers down the statue's weathered arm. 'Some of my bridge partners now want for two of these.' He fixed Trent with his translucent stare. 'Others are dead.'

The Asian hangers-on in Monaco. They'd looked Thai or Malaysian, rather than Filipino, but de Witt had tentacles throughout the region. It amounted to nothing in itself, but the tip-off seemed more credible than von Schrader being on de Witt's payroll. It had come from the horse's mouth. Besides, he'd seen the way he'd made tea and mutilated his prize shrub. There no way he was still in the game.

Trent's phone rang. 'Sir, I'm with someone -'

'Oh yeah?' Kane laughed. 'Friend or foe?'

Trent watched the doctor pick his way around the toxic pond. He disappeared inside. 'Friend.'

'Well listen up, I've news. I gave Dave Chisolm a bell. He's done some digging.' Chisolm was Kane's old training college mate. He'd spent most of his career nicking fraudsters before retiring early. Since then he'd made a fortune providing consultancy to betting firms.

'Turns out there was a lot money coming in for Jackson,' Kane said. 'To win the Worlds. This was three months back. A huge spike down in Asia.'

Trent counted back. 'Which month?'

'Start of June.'

'When exactly? What day?'

'Hold on.' Kane rustled some paper. 'Week beginning

the 12th.'

The week after Vondell had set his world record in Eugene. It didn't make sense. The Panamanian was on fire. He'd been seeing Stocking for at least three months by then. The affair hadn't taken anything out of him. The very opposite, in fact.

'Are you sure?' Trent said. The security association Chisolm worked for had been set up by a network of bookies to protect market integrity. A more sophisticated, Europe-wide police system had been in the pipeline for years, only to be been mired in funding delays and technical hiccups. Masterson had reservations about using private intelligence, but Chisolm's tip-offs had been instrumental in helping nail the spot-fixing cricketers; he'd been Kane's go-to guy ever since.

'Dave don't piss about,' Kane said. 'Besides, you should have heard him. Almost shat himself when the graph spiked up. All chips on the American. Have been for months.'

'Just Asia?'

'Yup. South-East of. Though we ain't talking big bets - tens of thousands of diddy ones. But they add up large. Anyway, where you at?'

The Bashin line had come to nothing, Trent explained. He'd traced von Schrader to Suffolk. The elderly doctor was no more capable of running multiple doping programmes than lining up for that evening's heats. He also had no love for de Witt - and wanted redress.

'Sounds to me,' Trent added, 'that what we're looking for is some kind of syndicate boss. Someone with reach. With the muscle to keep things quiet?'

Kane mulled it over. 'Possibly. And if they were in league with de Witt -'

'Then you might very well be right.' The old man was coming out. 'Listen, I've gotta go.'

Von Schrader walked slowly across, looking pleased with himself. In his hands was a small gift box.

'A slice of traditional Linzertorte,' he said, offering Trent the box. 'My mother's recipe, though I experiment with plum butter. So much better than redcurrants.'

Trent accepted, gingerly.

'Let me guess - your boss? I could tell by the way you stiffened. You like to impress.' Von Schrader popped on the lid. 'You still have not told me why you need this information?'

'I'll let you know,' Trent said unconvincingly. He'd already made one promise to Vondell he wasn't sure he'd keep. He reached for the gate. 'Just to be clear, you're no longer involved with any doping programmes, right? I mean, you're no longer in contact with Maureece de Witt?'

Von Schrader nudged aside his pesticide tins. With a grin, he said, 'My kitchen is small, and my papers are my only friends. The few concoctions I work on are restricted to what is in your hand,' he flourished his arm, 'and what you see here, in the garden.'

Yellow patches bubbled on the pond. Trent was sure they weren't there before.

'You're asking whether I get lonely, no?' Von Schrader rounded the tins. He placed a hand on Trent's box. 'Well you should come and see me again, yes? Spend some time with David ...'

TWENTY-ONE

'Come on, Kane, leave it to the big boys. You've had your fun, yeah?'

Rabbatts squeezed Kane's shoulder. His sleeve rode up, flashing his giant TAG Heuer.

'Ten minutes,' Kane said. 'Where's the harm in that? The Berlin business, that's all we're after.'

The US team manager jogged across the blue track. Jackson had another series of interval sprints, he explained, then he'd be done.

Rabbatts. Some Hogwarts-of-a-school then Oxford, according to Kane. He'd made Chief Inspector by thirty-five, the only DCI Trent had ever known to wear a three-piece suit. They had the same estuary accent. Except Trent's was real.

'Gaines may have spoken about money,' Rabbatts said firmly. 'Jackson's a very wealthy man, as we know, and they were close friends. We're still working on robbery as the motive. The money these guys earn -'

'We shan't mention Gaines, son.' Kane returned the shoulder squeeze. 'Scout's honour.'

A phone bleeped. Rabbatts frisked his pockets. 'All

right, all right.' Something more important had come up. He said to Trent, 'I'll speak with the US team management. Ten minutes only. Or I'll be calling Masterson.'

The university's indoor training facility was the size of an aircraft hangar. The American team was out on the track practising relay handovers. The place reeked of rubber and Deep Heat, the whole set-up putting Vondell's pock-marked track out east to shame. By the far wall was a row of exercise machines draped in US flags, a string of motivational posters taped to the windows above. One had been torn down and replaced with a picture of Jad Gaines. Beneath it, a row of battery-powered candles flickered feebly beside sympathy notes. A shout or two of encouragement echoed down the hall, but the atmosphere was, understandably, sombre.

They walked over and read the cards.

'Can't imagine him here,' Kane said.

'Gaines?'

'No. Your Austrian doc. In this kind of environment. Not from what you said.'

Trent couldn't either. But he'd seen the pictures, in black and white.

'He's happy enough. Back home. With David.'

'David?'

'Don't ask.'

Jackson was having treatment at the end of the straight. Trent watched him interact with the others. If Coach asked him to do something, he'd do it. Otherwise he remained aloof. How much of it was down to his friend dying was hard to tell. He might be like that all the time. He was the team's star, after all.

Trent quizzed Kane about Castillo. He hadn't heard of him either, though he'd encountered similar shady figures in the past. During the cricket busts he'd investigated an Indian boss rumoured to be masterminding a global criminal enterprise, but he'd stayed out of reach in every country he'd been indicted. Even Interpol couldn't put a face to him. The nastiest stories came out of the Central and South American soccer leagues, where lower division players were routinely murdered for failing match fixers.

'Scary buggers,' Kane shuddered. 'Set up like drug cartels. Almost impossible to bust 'cos everything's on a need-to-know basis.' He nodded at Jackson. The session was winding up. 'As I say, if he don't squeal I'll tap up Interpol. Unless this Castillo's bought them off, too.'

The US team manager jogged over flanked by security, poker-faced secret service types the size of linebackers, each wearing a curly-wired earpiece. Unlike his Canadian friend, they wouldn't be wishing him a nice day, Trent guessed.

Jackson would speak to them in the locker room, the manager explained. Ten minutes and no more. He had a race to run.

They went inside. The American was slumped on a bench. Trent offered his condolences.

'I saw Jad Gaines in Berlin,' he said. 'Looked the kind of guy you'd want on your team.'

Jackson rubbed his eyes. 'Lead-off. Last leg. Whatever. Skinny fucker always brought it home.'

The manager stepped in. 'No questions about Jad Gaines. Not without Chief Inspector Rabbatts present.'

Jackson put his head in his hands. 'My brother, man.' He was shaking. 'Why would anyone -'

'We're looking at who might have wanted to cause him harm,' Trent said. 'Darius Vondell, too.'

Jackson jumped up. His bodyguard darted forward to restrain him. 'The punk let Jad drive that shit-box car! What the hell were they even doing out there?'

'That's what we're trying to find out,' Kane said.

The manager whispered in Jackson's ear. Jackson told him to go. He trudged out, eye-balling Kane. 'As I said, no questions about Jad Gaines.'

'So what you wanna know?' Jackson said. 'I got business

in four hours.'

'Where is Maureece de Witt?' Trent said.

Jackson got up.

'He ain't here.' He pulled a sweatshirt from his locker.

'Then where is he?' Kane said.

'He's a busy man.' One of the holdalls Trent remembered from the penthouse lay on a bench. Jackson stuffed it with gear. 'Doesn't always watch me run.' He dropped his drink bottle. 'Coming over for this one though. Yeah, tomorrow, I think.'

'So he's not here for the heats?' Trent said. 'He hasn't flown in already? To meet Gabrielle?'

Jackson slammed his locker. 'She ain't returned my calls. De Witt's tied up, I guess. I just focus on winning, okay?'

Kane rested on the door. 'Why don't you report her missing?'

'Say, you funny, man! She can take care of herself. She's a big girl.'

Trent dipped his hand in an ice bath. She was no longer with Jackson. She was no longer with Vondell. Keeping de Witt's machine well oiled seemed her priority.

'It's easy enough to check flight records,' he said. 'We can always find him that way. I don't suppose he mentioned a promotional event he might be doing? With Alexei Bashin?'

'You said this was about Berlin.'

'It is.' Trent glanced at the door. He wasn't going to mention this Castillo. Not until Kane had called Interpol. Besides, if he was the scary fucker von Schrader claimed, Jackson wouldn't answer more without his lawyer present. Or de Witt by his side. Though from his body language he seemed almost as afraid of the South African.

'So we done?' Jackson shouldered his bag.

Kane shrugged. He reached for his smokes. 'No. But you've a race to run.'

Jackson stopped at the door. 'Say, I heard Vondell quit

hospital?'

'You heard right,' Kane said. 'But he ain't gonna make any start line tonight. Seems like you're a shoe-in, my son.'

The door handle seemed to stick. Jackson stared at it. With a huff he grabbed his bodyguard and stormed out.

'He ain't giving him up,' Kane said, pulling out a cigarette.

'Who?'

'De Witt.'

'It's more complicated than that.' Someone wanted rid of Vondell. If Jackson was in on any conspiracy, he was doing a good job of hiding it. Though something wasn't right. Big-time athletes gushed about managers and coaches with a mixture of praise and respect. Jackson did neither.

'I checked today's press.' Trent said. 'Rumour's out now they're both seeing Stocking. You don't keep a lid on that stuff for long.'

'Bit odd though ain't it? Biggest showdown since Brazil and the tabloids have kept shtum until now?' Kane found his lighter. 'Anyway, you tracked her down?'

Trent hadn't. Neither had the Murder Investigation Team by the sounds of it. Who knew what alias - or phone - she was using now.

He kicked a spinning machine, sending the wheel into a blur. 'So, say de Witt's involved with this Castillo operation. Started when he put fights on out East. Now he branches out and they want a piece of his new pie.'

'He ain't got a pie. He's got Lemond Jackson.'

'He's the only sprinter an average Joe can name. That's a pretty big slice.'

Kane grinned. He tapped his cigarette against the box.

'Say some scam's cooked-up,' Trent went on, 'with big money coming in for Jackson, right when he looks vulnerable - straight after Vondell's stolen his world record? A lot people are wanting Bad Boy to lose. But then he doesn't look like losing. So Filipino boss sends word that

135

Vondell's going to have some little accident. Like necking a poisoned drink. But that fails to work. And then -'

'Hello! Slow down. You always do this - put two and two together and make five.'

Trent shut the door. Whatever motive Jackson might have for being involved, he surely wouldn't risk a world title. Stocking on the other hand ...

'She started seeing Vondell in March. From what I see, she's spent more time with de Witt than Jackson.'

'And?'

'Vondell travels without a manager. Even his crazy hangers-on have disappeared. Who else knew his movements?'

'You seriously think she's involved?' Kane chuckled. 'That she'd knock off her boyfriend? For what? You're having a laugh.'

If the Hôtel du Palais had never happened he'd have no qualms about pushing her as the linchpin of the whole conspiracy. He'd ignored that voice in his head, hearing only hers.

You should probably be going. Unless you've any more questions ...

'Besides,' Kane said, 'how would you prove it? The whole chain, I mean. You'd need evidence of the micro bets, chain of command, the lot. It'd take months. Why bother with some high-profile event when you can bribe some ringer in a minor soccer league? Malaysia. Columbia. Somewhere like that. A red card before half time. Concede a shed load of corners. Spot betting - that's where it's at. Under-the-radar stuff. And who says this El Castillo exists, anyway? You thought Doctor Feelgood was calling the shots, and look how that turned out.'

'Hey, there's no smoking in here!' A campus guard filled the doorway. They trooped out. Jackson was being mobbed by screaming school kids. A barrage of press was being held back, with cameras flashing away outside.

136

Kane's phone rang.

'Is he really? Well, it's handy he's here now.' He nudged Trent. 'It's Claire.' He nodded towards Jackson. 'Are you going to tell him, or shall I?'

'What?'

'Vondell.' Kane reached for his smoke. 'He's running.'

TWENTY-TWO

'I'm talking serious players! Guys who want to cause him harm. Vondell needs protection. He doesn't have his own people!'

The officer on the phone garbled something about Vondell being given a security detail. Once they'd interviewed him again, that is. Rabbatts was with a rep from the organisational committee as they spoke.

Trent felt like punching the wall. 'You mean no-one's collared him? Where's he been all day!? He's about to race!'

The same constable had been there when Trent had given his statement. Another yes-man building Rabbatts' empire. Whatever story the murder squad were pulling together, it was taking an age. The stadium was ringed with more security than the Palace of Westminster, but it didn't mean someone wouldn't have a go. He'd tried calling Vondell to tell him to watch his own back, again without reply.

He jumped on a tube to Piccadilly. The heat throbbed from the crowds. Statues dressed as athletes and Greek Gods, their faces painted red, white and blue, peppered Covent Garden piazza, while volunteers in sponsors' t-shirts directed people to the fanzones. He watched a group of Chinese tourists thumb excitedly through the championships programme. The buzz the organisers had hoped for had finally arrived. Lemond Jackson was on every poster from here to Stratford. But the public didn't know the half of it. And someone was determined to keep it that way.

His pocket vibrated. 'Lester, my man. What you got?'

Nick Lester. Classmate from the College of Policing. As ambitious as a tortoise, but could find a needle in a haystack.

'Not much, I'm afraid. She's in the West End, I can tell you that.' Lester tapped away. 'Very nice ... very nice indeed. Found some old pics of her here. Bikini modelling. Bali ... or Thailand, is it?'

Trent slunk into a theatre doorway. Lester was in Counter Terrorism. He should be working on his own cases, not tracing phones. He'd be in the shit if Masterson or his own guv found out. As would Trent, if he didn't pass Rabbatts the Castillo lead.

'You can't be any more specific?'

'It's too crowded. How many phones per square mile? Thousands.' He laughed. 'You're a dirty dog, Trent, you really are. Isn't this Rabbatts' case now? Does Kane know what you're up to?'

More shopping. Or an early meal before the heats. She might even be with de Witt. If she'd nothing to be guilty of she should be out there cheerleading from the stands, but no-one had seen her since the Bashin promo. Claire was already at the stadium in case Stocking did show up, but was being babysat by Rabbatts.

'Just let me know if she moves!' Trent yelled above the traffic.

'Sorry, mate,' Lester said. 'That's the last one for now. I've heard there's some race on!'

The giant curved billboard at the bottom of Shaftesbury

Avenue fizzed into blinding orange. A camera hurtled down the track, before the tiles exploded into a million pieces. Lemond Jackson's face stared impassively across the teeming intersection, prompting a party of teenagers to leap up from their open-top bus and applaud. The sprinter's arm flashed up to reveal his watch. The screen burst into tiny fragments once more, re-assembling to reveal the luxury brand's logo.

Trent stormed down to Leicester Square. A white stretched Hummer picked its way through the crowds. He felt like ripping the doors open to see if Stocking or de Witt were inside, only to be rescued from embarrassment by the prom night teens hanging from its windows.

A massive screen had been erected down one side of the piazza. He pushed through the throng, the smell of sweat and fried onions rising over the crowd. Shots of the packed stadium cut to footage from the warm-up track. Jackson and the other sprinters were prowling around, stretching and pretending not to notice one another.

His phone rang.

'Sir, what news? The race is about to -'

'Where you at?' Kane bawled above din.

'Leicester Square.' 'I'm in that sports bar. Bottom of Haymarket. I've got news on that burner.'

'I'm there in five.'

The bar was fit to burst. Every flag under the sun was draped around the drinkers glued to the screens. Kane was squashed in by a window. He passed Trent a beer.

'Jackson's through!' he shouted above the racket.

Trent swore. 'I've missed it?!'

'Barely broke sweat.'

'How quick?'

'Nothing special.'

'What about Vondell?'

'Up next.'

Kane dragged him to the terrace. 'Rabbatts called.

They've stripped that phone. Found some argument about payment. Right before the Vectra rammed them off. No question it was a hit - the guys were being paid.'

'Argument? About what?'

'Money. Don't say how much, though it was kicking right off. Percentage up front, the rest after. Some disagreement about timing, too. Seems it almost broke down.'

'Who's the phone registered to?'

'Burner, as you said. Rabbatts' team: they ain't got a clue. No idea who the attacker was speaking with, neither.'

Trent fumed. They'd take another day to sort out the trace. Lester could do it in minutes.

'These texts - do they mention Vondell?'

'No. They might lose a phone, but they're too clever for that.'

A cheer rang out. Vondell was stripping off.

'Rabbatts volunteered all this?'

'Guessing Masterson's given him a slap-down.'

They edged back inside. Kane had called Interpol. The name Castillo had been hovering around for thirty years without any real evidence. Any decent leads had been silenced further down the food chain. It didn't mean he didn't exist. It just meant they'd need a skip-load of evidence to prove it. Kane was as sceptical of the Castillo line as he'd been about von Schrader. But the Austrian had been candid enough about de Witt. There was no reason to doubt him.

'I also called Border Force,' Kane said. 'Lady-Miss-Ten-Phones ain't left the country. And the two hotels she's supposedly been swanning in and out of: they checked 'em on CCTV. She ain't been to neither. Not since you saw her last.'

Trent nodded at the screen. 'They're lining up.'

Kane shook his head. 'Ha ha. You never let 'em go.' He waved his beer at the TV. 'She's probably down there right now. Handing out bouquets. You wouldn't put it past her.'

Trent wouldn't. Nor could he hide his embarrassment at letting her get under his skin. The fact that Kane had made more progress than him on her whereabouts also pissed him off. Like his dad had done his homework. At least he'd corroborated Lester's trace.

A wall of crowd noise swamped Vondell's introduction. The bar responded with a volley of 'C'mons!', peppered by drunken jeers. The Panamanian executed his trademark explosive start, taking a three-metre lead, only to be overtaken by Olivier Dufort at half way. The Frenchman relaxed into his stride, the flashbulbs propelling him to the line.

Vondell grimaced as he tightened up, finishing just ahead of the Brit next door. An intake of breath rippled the room.

Kane slapped Trent's shoulder. 'Lucky bastard!' Only the first two went through to tomorrow's semis by right.

Trent clocked the time. '9.97.'

'For Dufort,' Kane said. The results were confirmed. Vondell was second, in 10.10. 'He ain't winning diddly-squat with that.'

Vondell ripped off his shoes. He hurled his flowers into the crowd and headed for the mixed zone. A black tube bandage covered part of his snake tattoo. He wasn't the type to show pain, though he hadn't run well. Whether his injured arm was the reason, only he knew.

'One minute.' Trent's phone was vibrating. He stepped outside. 'Jay Trent.'

'Sergeant Trent, I do hope you remember me: it's *Kriminalkommissar* Daniel Krentz.'

'Krentz, hi. Look, I'm watching -'

'I've some bad news.'

The Hummer had wound its way down Haymarket. A blonde of sixteen or seventeen emerged from the sunroof. She clocked Trent and stuck out her tongue, capturing a selfie to a roar of approval.

'My colleague Hans Schönleber,' Krentz said, his voice wavering. 'He's had an accident. Climbing. In the Black Forest ...'

TWENTY-THREE

'Okay. Well if he turns up tell him Frank Kane wants a word.' Kane slammed down the phone. 'Zimmerman still out the office. God knows where.'

'Who was that?'

'Krentz again. No improvement in Schönleber. Still in intensive care.'

Trent swilled his coffee. Kane had hounded Zimmerman all evening after leaving the sports bar, only for Krentz to answer each time. Zimmerman was out: investigating Schönleber's accident, the Germans assumed, though he hadn't been seen since yesterday.

Someone had switched on the office TV. A couple of station cleaners had joined others watching the preliminary round of the pole vault, the last event of the afternoon's competition. The track, ringed by a capacity crowd, shimmered like a griddle pan. It was going to be even hotter that evening, with fast times promised.

Trent tried Schönleber again, only to get his voicemail. Besides head injuries, the poor guy had punctured a lung and broken a leg in the 20-metre fall. The doctors had deliberated about whether to induce a coma, deciding against it after he'd managed a whisper. Local police were investigating after his rope had been found shredded, the episode being treated as a tragic kit malfunction.

Kane had called Rabbatts to tell him he was trying to get hold of Zimmerman, but Rabbatts still wasn't interested: they had a murder to solve, the forensics still being their best lead. Trent spent another ten minutes arguing why they needed to be up in Silver Command, the ops room where Rabbatts' team was based, that evening.

'Hey, Trent.' Priestland was reading in Trent's chair, his feet up on the desk. 'What's this about your German? The spanner fell off a cliff?'

Trent flicked on a fan. It whirred into life before cutting out.

'Here -' Priestland held up his book. 'You should read this. Make up for what you've missed.'

It was the crammer Claire suggested.

'Move please.'

Priestland pushed himself away.

'How's the Breton case?' Trent said, logging in. 'I heard Redstone's making inroads. You owe him. And Claire.'

Priestland was younger than Trent by a couple of years and had just made sergeant. Masterson rated him too, despite him getting on Kane's tits. He'd also skipped his two years on the beat: something Trent never let him forget.

The Welshman sat back. 'Charged the stud owner last night,' he grinned. 'While you were out boozing.'

Trent called up Stocking's file. He'd already been through the news coverage on her marriage and the column inches devoted to her charity work. Truth be told, he didn't know what he was looking for. But there was something missing. Even if she was capable of having her lover killed, she couldn't have acted alone. There was something deeper between her and de Witt. The way they spoke: like she was his daughter. Jackson made all the money, but he was like

145

the unloved son, scared of letting down an abusive father.

He delved further into her career. Her teen modelling work in London had taken off after she'd been spotted by a fashion magazine. A New York agency had signed her up soon after, but the arrangement hadn't lasted, and she was soon back in England studying for a marketing diploma. The trail then seemed to go dead, before she turned up in Hong Kong. A luxury car manufacturer had launched in the city, one of the first big deals after the Chinese handover.

Clips of the event showed Stocking flanking the CEO at a ribbon-cutting ceremony. Her name was listed first in the caption, above all the back-slapping suits lined up on the stanchion. He found a longer video clip, the ad reps and trade delegates crowding her like bears eyeing a fawn.

Joining CEO Troy Roberts was Gabrielle Leech. The model has just signed a multi-million dollar contract to be the face of the company in Asia-Pacific ...

Spotlights fizzed over the assembly. He scanned the suits.

Then he saw him.

He rewound the clip. Slowing the footage, he waited for the lights to fall on the group to her right. The hair was thicker, the waistline smaller, but the drooping moustache was still the same.

De Witt.

A cheer went up from the corner of the office. A pole vaulter was back flipping after clearing the bar.

'Her third attempt!' Claire said, peering over his shoulder. 'She nearly blew it.'

Trent snatched up the crammer.

'What's that?' She nodded at the screen.

'Nothing.'

'Her again. You know, should do as he says.' She gestured at Priestland.

'What?'

'Get stuck into that.' She meant the book.

146

'What else you got on Gaines ...' He was distracted by Kane, who was on the phone. Masterson again, by the sound of it. '... I asked you to find out more.'

'There's nothing more than I told you.'

'What about Rabbatts? Did he say anything at the stadium?'

'No. They never tell me anything. Look, do you want the book or not?'

They never tell me anything.

'Trent?'

'What?'

'Trent, I said do you want the book or not?'

'Later. Sir!' Kane was leaving. Trent ran over. He caught him outside. 'Sir - about Schönleber -'

'Let me guess, you wanna send him flowers? Well you can't. Budget's blown as it is.'

'When he appeared in Monaco - how he just turned up, without telling us. No call from Zimmermann, nothing.'

'And?'

'Schönleber had been there, at the auction. He saw me and said zilch. So what if he wasn't there to spy on de Witt after all? What if he was keeping tabs on me?'

Kane scoffed. 'And he kept up the act? I doubt it. Don't sound the sharpest tool in the box.'

The crowd whooped in the office. A Brit heptathlete had just won the hurdles.

'And the official -' Trent went on, 'the one who retracted her complaint -'

'So Zimmerman's bent?' Kane started off down the corridor. 'If Masterson heard -'

'De Witt could have bought him off. Used him to keep Castillo off the radar. In Europe, at least.'

Kane fingered his stubble. 'Has Schönleber called you? Since you saw him last?'

'No. But Zimmerman doesn't know what we know. I spent time with the kid. They kept him in the dark. If he

147

knew too much -'

'Someone might arrange for his climbing rope to be cut?' Kane shook his head. He reached for his smokes. 'Look, we don't know Zimmerman from Adam.'

'Interpol do. And didn't Dave Chisolm have dealings? In Munich - some wonky player transfer?'

Kane slumped against the wall. 'So you want me to call Interpol again? And say what? "Berlin chief of police's taking backhanders from some race fixing scam"? Masterson'll have me crucified.'

'Then speak to her first. Or Chisolm.'

Kane gave him the look. Like he'd pitched another crazy plot. Though this time he wasn't laughing. 'I'll speak to Dave. You get yourself home. I'll see you at the stadium. I just spoke to Masterson. She don't want us pissing on Rabbatts. We'll be there tonight to observe, nothing more. Her orders. Let me call Dave Chisolm - we'll take it from there.'

'Yes sir.'

The guys watching TV quizzed him for more on the Gaines case. Trent made his excuses to leave, only to catch the fuzzy screengrab of Stocking still up on his monitor. He dived over and turned it off, before Claire could see.

Schönleber was safe in hospital. Vondell, if he made it through the semis, was about to run the biggest race of his life.

If he made it to the starting line.

TWENTY-FOUR

The athletes crowded the Gatorade bin like gazelles around a watering hole. 1500m runners awaiting their heats. High jumpers glancing warily at rivals. The few that weren't surfing on adrenaline were glugging their drinks, as if hydration alone would win them gold.

No-one escaped the heat. The warm-up track offered no shade. Soon they'd step from the fireside into the cauldron, the sun setting on the dreams of the weak-minded well before it sank over London.

Trent ripped off his hoodie. He'd come in jeans and a t-shirt, a poor disguise amid the blazered officials. He stood out like Jackson in Berlin.

Geary, one of Rabbatts' bag carriers, clocked him coming in and demanded he report to the ops room. Trent ignored him, harassing every steward and security guy until he'd located Vondell and Jackson. He'd precisely ten minutes until Rabbatts or Masterson turfed him out. Which was fine - Vondell's semi went off just after 7pm.

Jackson was doing knee lifts to the far side of the track. Vondell was stripped to the waist again, a sweating pack of muscle. The American's entourage bridled like angry bison each time he jogged by. A pair of uniformed police stood watching like fans at a meet-and-greet. There was no public access to the warm-up track, and the media was banned from the evening sessions. If Jackson had anything to do with the failed attempt on Vondell's life, there was nothing he or his people could do here apart from wish him a torn hamstring. Even so, the hair on Trent's neck stood up every time the Panamanian came around. Someone, very badly, wanted him to lose. Stadium security was tight, but a violent individual could always slip through.

The two men stalked the burnt orange oval like cheetahs in a cage. Trent scanned the lighting rigs. CCTV fed straight back to Silver Command, but it hardly mattered. Geary would have grassed him up by now.

A royal blue steward's blazer hung off a sand rake. Trent slipped it on. He crossed the hoarding and moved smartly across the outfield. He got within twenty feet of Jackson before the US team manager clocked him.

'The police officer, right?'

Trent pushed by.

'Hey! We said everything this afternoon.' He grabbed Trent's arm. 'Does Chief Inspector Rabbatts know -'

'One more question,' Trent said. 'We forgot something.'

Jackson's protection were being restrained by the Brit cops. One of the uniformed men reached for his radio as Jackson saw Trent.

'What you doin' wearing that shit?' Jackson pawed at Trent's blazer. 'Get the hell outta here! We done.'

'Gabby -'

'Say what?'

'Gabrielle. When did she and de Witt start working? I mean, before you two got together?'

The team manager intervened. 'This is right outta line. Lemond's about to compete -'

A uniformed officer stepped in. Trent lied about being on Rabbatts' instructions. The team manager butted in

150

again, haranguing the constable about repeated intrusion.

Trent collared Jackson. 'I just need to know when they met.' He lowered his voice. 'When they first started working together.'

'So the witch doctor ain't here to send me lame!' Vondell broke from his jog. He pointed to the police. 'You gonna cuff me to my blocks, or your goons pop me now?'

Jackson shoved him in the chest. Vondell stumbled and swiped with his fist, prompting the uniformed men to wade in.

'Away!' Trent threw off the blazer. He pushed Vondell back. 'You're on a charge, remember?'

'Yeah, get the hell outta here,' Jackson mocked.

'Fuck you, man!' Vondell chopped the air with his snake arm. 'He asked about Gabrielle, yeah? Say she lyin' in my crib right now, yeah? What she say about you? The press go ape shit if they knew the truth.'

Jackson edged around his manager, who was failing to hold him back. 'Yeah, fuck you too, loser.'

'You the loser. You be seein' my ass tonight. Nothin' else.'

'I said enough!' Trent spoke to the uniformed cops. They pulled Jackson and his party aside. Vondell, sensing he'd landed a blow, was already halfway around the track. 'Hey, Lemond!' Trent ran back to the group. The manager started on the uniformed men, demanding they take Trent away.

'It's ok.' Jackson mopped his head. 'One question. Then get this fucker outta here.'

'When did Gabby first work with de Witt?' Trent said. 'That's all I want to know.'

Jackson shrugged. 'I dunno. Way back. We met in Dallas ... before that -' He shook his head. 'She was in Europe. But earlier ... hell knows ... Asia?'

'Asia? Where in Asia?'

'Tokyo. Kuala Lumpur. She talked a lot about Hong

151

Kong.'

There would be no reconciliation. The way Jackson talked she was already ancient history.

'What did she do there? For de Witt?' Trent's heart pumped. 'Modelling, but what else? Before the de Witt Foundation -'

'Hey that's enough!' The huge protection guy who'd done his best to intimidate the Germans muscled in. 'We're done with questions!'

'Yeah we done.' Jackson snapped on his headphones. 'I know shit before we got together. And I don't know shit where she is now.'

Some of Rabbatts' other officers were clambering over the hoarding. Vondell had reached the back straight and was stretching. Trent needed more. But his time was almost up.

He went to shake Jackson's hand, but he was already jogging away. Pinned to his number, Trent saw, was a tiny photo of Jad Gaines.

The first semi was called in. Trent sprinted over to Vondell.

'You didn't back me up,' Vondell shouted above the stadium roar. 'About the doctor. Dr Dope.'

'You shouldn't have mentioned it. You had no right -'

Vondell pulled out some pins. He skewered his race number. 'God forbid I say something *controversial*. And after what the media done to me?!' He squeezed into his vest. He looked a foot smaller, as if shrunken by the spat. 'Say, what you found out about Berlin? You got my number.'

'I'm working on it.'

'Yeah, well.' Vondell searched the track. The fire from his eyes had gone, replaced by something else entirely. For the first time, the World's Fastest Man looked scared.

'What did the officers say about your security - the ones by the track?'

'They ain't said nothin'.'

'Then how did you get here?'

'Called me a cab. I ain't got no wheels.'

Trent cursed. Rabbatts had left him to fend for himself. Still working on the robbery theory, despite the mounting evidence.

The others competitors were entering the call room. Vondell took a final drink.

'You prepare that yourself?' Trent said, watching him sink the purple liquid.

Vondell rotated the bottle, like a flask in a lab.

'Why?' He nodded in Jackson's direction. 'You think he spiked me again?'

Trent held his tongue. 'I don't know. I wondered if Gabby had mixed it.'

Vondell hurled the bottle away. 'I told you, man, she's gone!'

'That's not what you just said to Jackson.'

'Say any shit to wind him up.'

'You don't have to do this.'

Vondell puffed out his barrel chest. 'Jackson calls it business. Well, this time I'm bankrupting the motherfucker.'

An official by the entrance was counting in the runners. Behind him the call room tunnel gaped like a black hole.

'You know she said she'd be here.' Vondell looked up at the tangle of steel cables feeding the replay screen. He shook his head. 'All the macho stuff … all the bullshit … that ain't real, man. But what me and her had together, what we shared … hell, she said she'd look out for me. And I believed that crap.'

So it had meant something. Behind all the trash talk and muscle was the need to be wanted. He was just like Jackson. Stocking. Maybe all of us.

One of Jackson's bodyguards cat-called, making some obscene gesture. Vondell flexed his mountainous deltoids, snapping quickly back into role.

'You said you'd help me.' His eyes bored into Trent. The

153

race-face was back.

'I'm doing all I can.' Rabbatts was running out of the tunnel. Behind him was Kane, stumbling to keep up. 'Good luck.'

'I don't need no luck.'

TWENTY-FIVE

'Get out!'

Geary, Rabbatts' gopher who'd warned Trent earlier, sloped out into the corridor. His boss stood with Masterson, arms folded, against the window overlooking the stadium. It looked like an interrogation. Which was what Trent was about to get.

'This is totally against protocol!' Masterson shouted. 'You posed as an official to reach Lemond Jackson, when you'd already spoken with him this afternoon. Why?'

A fanfare announced Vondell's semi. It was now about the Panamanian, Trent explained: he'd come to warn him to be careful. Without adequate protection -

A roar went up. The crowd rose as one, springing Trent from his seat.

'Sit down!' Masterson thrust out a palm. 'Chief Inspector Rabbatts is handling Jad Gaines' murder. I told Kane that you were to help the Germans with the Berlin investigation. Nothing more.'

Kane was red-faced against a Post-It board. He'd also been given a bollocking, but Trent knew he was more to blame. He hadn't given Kane enough. Forget about getting that scally Lester into trouble; he was on the verge of costing Kane his badge.

'We received a written complaint this afternoon,' Rabbatts said, brandishing a letter. He sat on a chair backwards, like a drama teacher. 'From Jackson's management - before you muscled in this evening. Says you've made a series of approaches to Lemond. All unauthorised.'

Masterson snatched the letter. 'You realise this is harassment? I could lose my job for this!' She slapped it down. She was usually the firm-but-fair type - Trent had never seen her like this.

'They weren't all unauthorised, ma'am. They invited me - to Monaco -'

'I sent you home!' Kane picked up the note. 'You were leaving it me - to speak to Dave Chisolm, remember?' He had his back to the Masterson. He glared and raised his brow. It took a moment for Trent to cotton on. Kane had told her about his stay in Monaco. Though she evidently hadn't seen the budget sheet. 'Can we get some air in here?' Kane wrenched at his collar. 'I'm sweating like a nonce in Mothercare.'

In lane four, representing Panama, world record holder and current Pan-American champion, Darius Vondell!

Trent shot to the window. The cheers from the crowd just about outnumbered the boos. Vondell looked mean, squatting and leaping like a jack-in-a box. Trent's eyes raced over the camera flashes. He'd at least be running his semi, or so it seemed. It would take a sniper pointing down his lane to ...

'He can't win,' Trent said, his throat bone-dry. He pointed down the track. 'They don't want him to win. He can't make the final!'

'Who can't?' Masterson said.

'Vondell! He's in danger! Don't you see?' Trent stuck his nose to the window. The athletes were called to their

156

blocks.

Then silence. Masterson, Rabbatts and Kane craned their heads round to watch.

Set.

The gun fired. Trent's heart hit the roof. A thousand flash bulbs blinded him to the stands. Vondell was already at forty metres. In a blur of glistening limbs he streaked ahead of the two Jamaicans. With twenty metres left he eased down. Crossing the line he raised his finger, some gesture, apparently, to the press box.

'Whoa! 9.78!' Kane clapped Trent's shoulder. 'Our man - he's back!'

Masterson's look hadn't changed. If anything she looked even more unimpressed.

Rabbatts whispered in her ear.

'You're meant to be on leave, Trent,' Masterson said. 'Preparing for your inspector's exam. Is that correct?'

'Ma'am, I don't know what Kane has told you, but Darius Vondell needs armed protection, right now -'

He blurted out the conspiracy. Castillo. How de Witt was on his payroll. Jackson might not be in on it, but Stocking certainly was. They needed to find her. Fast. But the priority was Vondell.

Rabbatts grunted. 'Ma'am, we've the forensics on the burner phone, we can't afford -'

'Berlin -' Trent said, 'Vondell's poisoning, it was real. The officer assigned - Schönleber - he was there to keep tabs on me. They're in the pocket of de Witt -'

A smirk crossed Rabbatt's lips. 'This is all news to me, ma'am. If any evidence -'

'I tried to tell you!' Trent said. 'They didn't -'

'Stop!' Masterson glared at Kane. 'Why wasn't I told any of this earlier?' Kane tried to speak but she hadn't finished with Trent. 'Go home immediately. Get back to your books. I hardly need to say that all this looks very bad indeed. Kane, we need to talk. I want a full debrief on what

157

you and Trent have been up to, not the crap you gave me on the phone. In the meantime, no-one's to speak with Rabbatts' team. Do you understand?'

Kane's phone rang. He slipped behind the pinboard.

'You've been watching too much TV, mate.' Rabbatts patted Trent's arm. 'It don't work like that. Not in the real world. It's all about procedure. You take a lie down, yeah?'

Trent argued with him before Masterson cut them off. 'Who's your CO, Rabbatts? I need a word.'

'Culverhouse.'

Kane returned, coughing loudly. He looked like he'd seen a ghost.

'Did you hear what I said?' Masterson planted the complaint letter on Kane's chest. 'About Rabbatts' team: no one's to -'

'That was Berlin,' Kane said.

'What?'

'Krentz. Their second-in-command.'

'And?'

Kane turned to Trent. 'Zimmerman. He's been arrested. Trying to fly out of Dusseldorf.'

'Arrested?!' Trent said. 'On what charge?'

The Americans' complaint letter was on the floor. Kane stuffed it in Rabbatts' hand. 'Suspicion of taking bribes, accessory to attempted murder and gambling fraud.'

The stadium roared as the second semi was announced. Masterson glanced outside. A film of condensation was forming on the window.

'Ma'am,' Kane said, 'with your permission, I need Trent -'

'I want to know who you've spoken to,' Masterson said, 'and when. The lot. Right now!' She opened the door. 'Rabbatts, tell Chief Superintendent Culverhouse I want him.'

'But ma'am, he told us to -'

'Just do it!'

He slunk out.

'I'm a mug. They mugged us off!' Kane booted the nearest table. 'Zimmerman ... we were helping him out!'

Trent jabbed the pinboard. 'So they think he arranged Schönleber's fall?'

'And the rest. They've got decent evidence, too: a betting syndicate. Thousands of punts on Jackson. Spread out over the summer. David-Clever-Bastard-Chisolm. I told you he'd come good. They've put a warrant out for de Witt.'

The thought of Berlin made Trent's stomach heave. He'd been their stooge all along. Though whatever had happened to that fool Schönleber, he hadn't deserved it. The poor bugger had been a pawn in it all. Just like him.

Masterson jabbed her phone. 'Who picked up Zimmerman?'

Kane groped for a smoke. 'Their border police.'

'We need to speak to Interpol.'

'Have done.'

'What do you mean "you have done"?! About what?'

'This Castillo. They reckon he's done a Lord Lucan. Either that or he never existed.'

'Damn it!' Masterson threw down her phone. 'I'll speak to my contact there about de Witt. I want you and Claire to find him - we need him in right now. He's the best lead to Stocking.'

'He should have flown in,' Trent said. 'Jackson said so.'

'Right, well get on it. I'll ask Culverhouse to release some of Rabbatts' team. And this Krentz's number - I'll need that too. You,' she poked Trent, 'take an officer from outside and protect Vondell. I want him here under armed guard. He doesn't leave the stadium unless I say so.'

'Yes ma'am.' Trent sprinted to the door.

'And Trent -'

'Ma'am?'

'You'd better be right.'

TWENTY-SIX

U-S-A!, U-S-A!

Jackson fans draped in the stars-and-stripes were leaping from their seats. Trent cut through and dashed down the staircase. The stadium was full, even the VIP sections. Above the corporate boxes the structure's giant stanchions stabbed skywards like claws, as if fearing a threat from above.

He flashed his badge halfway down the stand. The steward was explaining the quickest route to the warm-up track when an arena-rumbling fanfare crescendoed. The floodlights went out. Dozens of spots raced over the outfield, before converging on the start line.

'Sir, as I say, you want to take staircase F, cutting through the mixed zone - you'll need your police accreditation.'

Trent leaned over the barrier. A roar went up as Jackson filled the giant screen. He stalked forward in his lane, tall and lean, firing his fingers like pistols. The other sprinters threw their own moves, before the starter called them forward.

Trent's phone vibrated. It was Kane.

An ear-piercing *sssh!* came over the PA. They'd gone five metres before most of the crowd heard the gun. The arc of noise all but blew Trent down the stairwell. Jackson made a better start than usual, maintaining his drive phase for fifty metres.

By the time he'd lifted his head, the race was won. With ten metres left, the Dutch champion moved up into second and beamed across, but the American wasn't up for showboating. His business was done.

'9.78!' The steward yelled. 'Yeah! Him and Vondell - they done the same time!'

Trent watched the screen. The first five rows on the bend surged forward. Jackson decelerated to a jog, ignoring calls for autographs.

'Damn it!' He'd missed Kane's call.

The screen flashed to the triple-jump. An athlete was trying to harness the crowd, who were still fixated on Jackson. The camera panned left along the back straight, picking out more screaming fans.

'Wait!'

Trent shook his phone at the screen.

'Hey!' He grabbed the steward. 'Did you see that -'

He swiped a woman's binoculars. 'I need to borrow those. One second.'

'Hey sir!' The steward stepped in, 'you can't just -'

Trent ran down the steps. The triple-jumper was hurtling down the runway. Behind him spectators were fanning themselves, unable to take their eyes off Jackson.

'Sir, can you give those back to the lady -'

A string of media boxes were perched above Row Z. Beneath them, a single steward sat amongst a handful of empty seats. To his right, a group of mean-looking men in t-shirts seemed more interested in the spectators than the action.

Amidst them, sitting brazenly in a Hawaiian shirt and slacks, was Maureece de Witt.

161

Trent looked away. Two more security guards were coming. He tossed them the binoculars back and called Masterson.

'Ma'am, it's Trent.'

'Do you have him?'

'Who?'

'Vondell, for chrissake! Is he under guard?'

'Ma'am, I'm in the stands. You're not going to believe this - he's here!'

'Who's here?'

'Maureece de Witt!'

The floodlights went down for the next event. Trent searched the stand. The South African was still there, but some of the Russians were on the move.

Masterson hesitated. 'Who's he with?'

'Usual entourage. Well, some of them: the MMA guys, definitely.'

'Where exactly?'

'Above the back straight. Almost the last row. Hell knows why he's up there. If he's the balls to turn up he could at least sit in VIP.'

'The stadium map ...' Masterson scratched around. 'Let me speak to Rabbatts. See how Culverhouse wants to play it.'

'But ma'am -'

'I'll call you back.'

The women were coming out for the 10,000m final. Trent raced up the stairwell. The big screen focussed in on the runners. He tried to call Kane but got no response. De Witt's group were almost in shadow. Others were leaving. If the South African had risked coming here, he'd surely stay for the final. But he was as elusive as Stocking. And there was the little matter of a world title fight that night.

'Yes ma'am?'

'Is he still there?' Masterson's voice wavered.

'Yes. Should I bring him in?'

162

'No.'

She spoke heatedly with a group, Rabbatts among them. 'Look .... this could get messy. We need more time. Keep eyes-on.'

'But ma'am -'

'There's two of you, isn't there? I asked you to take somebody.'

Trent looked round. Above him the security guys glared from the steps. 'Uh-huh.'

'Good. Then await my orders.'

'What about Vondell?'

'I'll have Rabbatts send more men.'

'Damn it!' Trent shielded his eyes. The lights fell on the women preparing to race, shrouding the opposite stand further in shadow. There was no way he could lose de Witt now. They might not have enough to arrest him tonight, but he'd surely know where Stocking was. It might be all they need.

He grabbed the steward. 'What's the fastest way over there,' he pointed across the outfield, '- the block across the way?'

'Why you wanna know?' One of the other guards stepped in.

Trent flashed his badge. The steward apologised. 'Sorry, officer. I thought you wanted the athletes' area?'

'I did.'

'Down these steps. Show your accreditation at checkpoint B and go through the door. Follow it down into the parking lot. Cross all the way over to service stairwell G. It'll take you right up behind block 236.'

'Thanks.' Trent tore down the steps.

'Do you need help, sir? I can call for backup ...'

TWENTY-SEVEN

His footsteps echoed like gunshots. Despite being only feet behind the plush hospitality suites, the stairwell was as grey and cold as an abandoned factory.

Three floors down the stadium noise faded. The only noise was a low hum from the heating vents. Trent followed the floor lights to the parking lot. Luxury cars and hire vehicles filled every space.

As he searched for the right exit a blast from a vent scorched his neck. De Witt didn't do public transport. Somewhere here was his ride. If he was planning on making the Munich fight, he was cutting it fine. Though he'd risked enough already. He surely wouldn't miss Jackson's final.

He cut between two Range Rovers. A yellow exit sign glowed dimly in the corner. He was starting towards it when something struck him hard on the shoulder.

He fell forward, his face hitting the radiator of a Mercedes. The blow seared through his temple. He cried out, only for a punch to sent him reeling under the tyres.

A pair of Chelsea boots stopped by the fender. Trent coughed, his mouth sticky with blood. He tried to roll out, but a boot kicked him over again. The smell of oil stung his nose. A car unlocked with a blip. The blow to his head had tilted the world, as if the vehicles, stadium and all of its spectators were sliding into a giant sinkhole, the clip endlessly replayed in the Mercedes' undercarriage. He saw Jad Gaines' wrecked car, the sprinter bloodied and limp against the door like a tortured doll. This time, however, it was not Vondell at the wheel, but Gabrielle Stocking, her head thrown back in abandon as she pitched them into the abyss.

His attacker was returning. Trent's cheek met the concrete. One leg of his assailant's pinstripe suit had lodged in a boot. The trousers were too small, Trent noticed, as a pair of gloves grabbed his ankles. Before he could see his attacker's face, he was dragged out and forced onto the car's hood. Cheap aftershave and sweat replaced the stench of oil. He tried to wrench himself free, but his right arm felt bruised and lame.

'Who the -'

A hand cuffed his head. His chin met the cold metal. In the windshield he caught a glimpse of the besuited man tethering his hands. Stocky, with hair slicked back, he went about his work with a butcher's hands.

'I'm a police officer!' Trent mouthed, his split lip against the hood.

A screech of tyres bounced off the walls. The face in the window looked up. Seeing his chance Trent kicked like a mule, then smashed his elbow into the man's chest.

A pair of headlights flashed. Trent rolled away. He picked himself up as his attacker lunged again.

Schalk!

De Witt's henchman aimed a fist at his jaw. Trent lurched backwards, his arm throbbing as it crumpled. A car door slammed.

'Trent! Roll away!'

It was Claire. She jumped onto Schalk's back, shoving his face to the ground. The South African swore as she

165

twisted his arm up his spine. Trent pinned his legs.

'De Witt will kill you for his,' Schalk growled, dark blood trickling from his temple. 'The bitch too!'

'The bitch has you under arrest.' Claire wrenched his other arm around. She cuffed him and read his rights.

'Get him up.' Trent wiped his mouth.

De Witt's sidekick looked faintly ridiculous in the pinstripe, his thighs stuffed in like sandbags. The powder blue suit, he guessed, must be at the cleaners.

They pushed him against a pillar. He was carrying nothing but a phone.

Trent rummaged in his own pockets for some paper.

'Here,' he handed Claire a note. 'Call this.'

'What -'

'The burner I found at Jad Gaines' crash. The texts went to this number.'

'We can't -'

'Just do it.'

Schalk panted. A smirk grew across his face as a cheer penetrated from above. Less than thirty minutes until the final. Rabbatts would have to take Schalk in: they needed to get back up there. Find Vondell - and fast.

Claire looked around. She rang the number. The screen on Schalk's phone seemed to fade. It turned white.

Then it rang.

The number was his.

'De Witt -' Trent said, forcing Schalk back against the pillar. 'Why did he order the hit on Vondell?'

Schalk laughed. 'You really are an amateur. A fucking lightweight. Just like your girlfriend here.'

Claire twisted his arms. He snarled as the cuffs cut his wrists.

As he tried to turn, a key fob fell from his trousers. Trent picked it up. He pressed the button. Schalk tried to bolt. They wrenched him to the ground. Trent tried the button again. This time a car blipped. By an pillar opposite, something glowed.

Claire nodded. 'The 4x4. Over there -'

'Let me speak with Chief Inspector Rabbatts,' Schalk gasped, rolling over like a dead weight. 'I need to speak with Chief Inspector Rabbatts!'

They hauled him up. His body went limp as they dragged him to the car. Trent pressed the fob again. It was another white 4x4 - the same or similar to the one Schalk had ridden in Monaco.

'Open it.' Trent spun him so his hands were by the trunk.

'You heard me,' Schalk said, his voice shaking. 'De Witt will have you killed for this!'

'So you've said. Now open it.'

The trunk sprung open. Inside were dozens of shoe boxes filled with documents. Beside them was a briefcase - the one Schalk had carried in Monte Carlo - and numerous pairs of men's shoes.

Trent opened the case. Inside was a laptop and more Drey-Bashin tickets.

'What's that?'

Schalk craned his head around. A long, leather-clad box was stuffed in behind the shoes. Trent picked it up. 'I said what -'

Schalk spat down Trent's shirt. Trent slammed him against the Cayenne next door. Schalk yowled as his head struck the window.

'Here -' Claire cuffed him to a fire hydrant.

Trent took out the long box. He flipped the catches.

Inside, separated into three parts, was a short-handled rifle, its telescopic sight snug in its velvet recess.

'So this is what you were coming for.' Trent picked up the gun. The insurance policy, should Vondell make the final. The perfect weapon for killing an athlete from distance, and discreet enough to conceal in the stand. Though how had they smuggled it in? There had to be an

167

insider. De Witt had bought off the Chief of Berlin police. Planting a ringer here was peanuts. Though hell knows how far up de Witt's tentacles reached. Hadn't Schalk mentioned Rabbatts … ?

Claire was phoning someone. She broke off. 'Rabbatts' team is heading down. Masterson wants you on Vondell. Now.'

Schalk kicked the 4x4. 'When de Witt sees Rabbatts -'

'You'll be in a cell.' Trent pointed to Claire's car. 'Let's get him in there.'

They dragged him over and locked him in, then returned to the Range Rover.

'Don't touch anything.' Trent grabbed Claire's arm.

He was about to close the trunk when a blast from a vent dislodged some paper.

Claire reached out. 'You said don't touch!'

Trent picked it up. It was a spreadsheet full of numbers, with words in an Eastern script. In the margins were scribbles in English. Dates. Locations.

Sporting fixtures.

He ripped the lids from the boxes.

'Trent! We need to find Vondell!'

He pulled out more sheets. Each had a column showing odds. Hundreds of names and addresses were listed on each sheet. Beside each was a figure in US dollars. All had the same date.

'This is it!' He ripped out more of the documents. 'They're betting receipts. For tonight's final!'

Claire looked down the lists. 'The words look Malaysian - or Thai, maybe. How can you tell?'

He sat on the hood of the car next door. Claire pulled out more boxes. Scores more receipts, with spreadsheets and emails in the same language. Micro-bets, extorted across Asia. They had to be.

Claire cocked her head incredulously. She reminded Trent of Stocking. 'So not only would de Witt risk everything by attending the murder of his star's greatest rival, he'd ride with enough evidence to sink Al Capone?'

'He doesn't do technology. Or so he says.' Trent glanced at the exits. He needed to speak to Kane. Get Dave Chisolm on it - and see what else Krentz had found. They had Schalk's phone. The rifle was more than enough to bring de Witt in. He might not fear the law, but they'd screwed up big time. Compared to what this Castillo might do, jail was nothing.

A muffled cry rose from Claire's car. Schalk was thumping a window, rocking it like a crib.

Trent slid off the hood. The car was dark grey, its near wing resprayed - badly - above a cracked headlight.

'You're kidding me -'

'What?'

He jumped down. The bodywork, at least what was visible beneath a thick film of dirt, was actually metallic black. He tried to look through the passenger window, but couldn't. That was tinted too.

'Trent?'

'It's the Vectra! The one that chased Gaines and Vondell!'

'How do you know?'

He checked the plates. Both were new. He looked through the windscreen. Inside was a carpet of litter: fast food wrappers and empty sports drinks. Forensics would need to sweep it, but he was ninety percent sure. De Witt had his posse of MMA guys protecting him in the stadium. It was they who'd chased Vondell and Gaines that night. He was sure of it.

One of the exits crashed open. Rabbatts, members of his team, and a pair of armed officers from SCO19, the specialist firearms unit, came tearing over.

Trent pocketed Schalk's phone.

'Trent!' Claire said. 'You should give that to Rabbatts!'

'And waste more time?' The final went off in an hour.

169

'This thing will be over by 10.' He stuffed the documents back. 'You impound the cars. I'll speak to Kane about these papers. If Masterson asks questions, tell her I'm with those guys.' He nodded at the armed officers. 'I'm going for Vondell.'

TWENTY-EIGHT

'Then where the hell is he?!'

Kane slapped the ops room window. Outside, the fans rose to salute the Kenyan 10,000m winner on her lap of honour. Trent watched her jog barefoot around the bend, waving her bouquet. He half expected Stocking to be in the front row, radioing Vondell's movements to de Witt. She'd slipped through his fingers. And now he'd lost them both.

He spoke to more of Rabbatts' team. An officer had seen Vondell heading for the locker room after his semi, but had lost him after being diverted to the parking lot. Trent had sprinted down to find the Dutch champion and other finalists joking in their ice baths. None of them had seen Vondell, either. Trent tried the warm-up track, called the Panamanian's hotel and tried his cell phone again, but there was no sign of him. Once more, he'd disappeared.

He dialled the private security hub. Athlete security was handled by another company, he was told. He'd need to speak with them.

Sweat dripped from his chin. He pressed his face to the window, frantically searching the mixed zone. Masterson was with Culverhouse and Rabbatts, dealing with Schalk and deciding what to do with de Witt. He was damn lucky she wasn't there.

'Jackson and his team manager,' he said to Kane, 'they're camped out on the warm-up track. I could -'

'You could tell Lemond that Bad Boy's gone AWOL and send de Witt scarpering to Munich. Proper screw us up!' Kane blew out his cheeks. 'For all we know Jackson's engineered the whole thing, killing his team mate in the process. At least with de Witt we're eyes-on. Claire's out there now.' He mopped his brow. 'Fuck me, I need a drink.'

De Witt was still wedged in his seat, his band of goons standing around like doormen. They looked twitchy. They'd be expecting Schalk back.

Trent gritted his teeth. He could charge up and take de Witt himself. He'd hardly pitch his men into a fight, not in front of the cameras. Though Kane was right. Until Masterson gave word, de Witt was free to stroll right out of the stadium and disappear off to Germany. And who knew who else he had hidden in the stands. Claire couldn't watch everyone.

'Anyway,' Kane rubbed his face, 'while you were dicking around downstairs, Masterson asked about someone called Annette - Stocking's assistant, and a couple of posers or hangers-on. Brothers, they reckon.'

Trent pricked up his ears. 'Her right-hand woman. And the twins - bag carriers, basically.'

'Yeah, well, they're down at Whitechapel now. Rabbatts' team brought them in. They want to know what they've seen, who Jackson's bird's been with. Though by the sounds of it that's half the locker room.'

Claire flew in. She dashed to the window. 'Sir, one of the knuckle-scrapers - he went to leave, but they called him back. De Witt's on and off the phone. He might be calling Schalk -'

She saw Trent skulking by the pinboard. 'Where's Vondell?!'

'Lost him,' he said, sheepishly. 'Last seen leaving the track.'

'He's running in forty minutes! What about the phone?'

Kane kicked the door shut. 'What phone?'

'You mean you haven't told him?!' Claire said.

Trent pulled it out. 'Schalk's. The whole conversation with the burner - it's all on there. They shifted the time of the hit - from 8.30 to 10.'

Kane put his head in his hands. 'You mean to say, you removed a phone from a key suspect without telling the Murder Investigation Team?' He shook his head. 'If this doesn't add up you are well and truly screwed. We all are. If Masterson walks in here now -'

'That and the boxes in the car,' Trent said, 'the betting evidence -'

'Whoa!' Kane said. 'Rabbatts mentioned boxes. He didn't say what was in 'em.'

Claire explained.

'They're written in Thai,' Trent said. 'Or Malaysian. Or something -'

'Or something? Fucking translator now are we?! Christ!' Kane ripped out a cigarette. Trent hadn't seen him this stressed since Janice left.

They told him about the betting receipts.

'I'll speak to Chisolm.' Kane tugged at his sweat-soaked collar. 'Get him to look at these boxes. Then I'll phone Krentz. See what Zimmerman's coughed up.'

Trent glanced at the clock. In just over half an hour Vondell would line up for the biggest ten seconds of his life. He wasn't warming up. Was he back with Stocking? Either that, or dead in the canal ...

The *Star Spangled Banner* drifted upwards. The American winner of the long jump stood atop the podium, his hand clasped to his chest.

Trent looked across the stadium. 'But why would he risk it? De Witt - coming here?'

'Shit the bed!' Kane cursed his phone. Chisolm wasn't answering.

'I mean, why would he parade in public, with all the security and police, when he surely knows we're on to him?'

'Ego.' Kane slapped his hands on the window. 'It's a performance, ain't it? The real big boys, playing in the big league - they're all as bent as him. Publicity. Profile. It's their lifeblood. They can't live without it. It's about them - not the athletes, not the talent. Sporting stars come and go. There's always another young fighter, another sprinter. They're just cash cows to leech off.'

'But he's out there now.'

'Too right. Sitting pretty. Who knows who's got his back? Zimmerman's in his pocket, we know that.' Kane threw an arm round the arena. 'And security here. Wouldn't take a king's ransom to buy someone off.'

Masterson was outside. She was bawling at someone - Culverhouse, Trent guessed.

Kane wiped his palm down the glass. It squealed like a pig. 'And then there's Castillo ...'

Trent's phone rang. They all stared at the number.

'It's Vondell.'

TWENTY-NINE

'Well, answer it!' Claire said.

'Jay Trent.'

Vondell was breathing hard. Running from an MMA goon? Or reeling beneath some crosshairs?

'Where are you?!' Trent said. A muffled hum filled the line. Traffic, it sounded like.

'By the river.'

'What the hell you doing there?! We've been ...' Trent stopped before mentioning Schalk. 'Look, we need you back in here. Now -'

'Ow! What the fuck -'

'Are you okay? Darius -'

'Jesus, it's dark.'

'Where are you exactly?' It sounded like he was jogging. The humming noise, Trent now realised, was the stadium crowd. He put Vondell on speaker.

'Across the river,' Vondell said. 'There's some old buildings. Factories or whatever. Kids eating outside.'

Claire shot to the opposite window. Fish Island. A row of abandoned wharves and other industrial units lining the far bank. Fancy apartments, with others converted into studios and restaurants, though the waste grounds were still a no-go at night. He had to be there.

Trent lowered his voice. 'Look, you're racing in thirty minutes. I'm pleading with you -'

'I ain't calling about that.'

'Go on.'

'That night at the track. When you were buggin' my ass. What I told you. Well I never told you the truth.'

'Which part?' The line went silent. 'Darius?'

He strained to get the words out. 'She asked me ... I mean she told me. That night ...'

'Who did?'

'Gabrielle.'

Across the river a light came on in one of the penthouses. A woman on her phone, Stocking's age or younger, walked out onto the balcony. She turned back, without a glance, as if the stadium wasn't there.

'She'd booked a table,' Vondell went on. 'Some smart restaurant in the mall. A private room. We were going to talk - sort things out. Make or break, you know?'

'And?'

He hesitated. 'She called me. Before you arrived. Pushed the table back ninety minutes.'

Trent nodded at Kane. 'Why? Weren't you with those jumpers? The Canadian women?'

'She pissed me off. What you saw at the track ... those women ... going with them was gonna be revenge, right?'

'For what?'

'Jackson. Gabby was gonna leave him. Before we came to London. Then it all went to shit. What Gaines said, in the car ...' His voice cracked. 'I said to myself, "no way". She wouldn't do it. Not to me. Not after what we had together ...'

Schalk's phone bulged in Trent's pocket. He stared into the black wastes of Fish Island. Vondell had no-one. He, more than Jackson or Stocking, even, needed to share. But he had fallen for the wrong person. He'd made his choice.

One that had almost killed him.

An SCO19 officer barged in. Kane pulled him over. They found Fish Island on the map.

'Look,' Trent said to Vondell, 'you're in real danger. You're safer inside the stadium. Besides, there's no point wasting energy on the past. We can protect you. If we can just get you to the call room -'

'Nah man, I ain't running.'

'But the time you ran earlier, in the semi -'

'Ain't doing it. It's gone, whatever.'

The woman in the penthouse re-appeared. A light had come on, casting her in silhouette, the phone still clamped to her ear. It was like Trent had seen her before.

'Jackson,' Trent said. 'He could be up to his neck in it. With her. They could have planned it all. Together.'

Claire glared at him. A roar went up in the stadium. The clock was ticking. Trent ran to the window. Beside a montage of Jackson and Vondell, a timer was counting down.

Vondell went quiet. 'You guarantee my security?' he said, eventually. 'I'm talking men with guns.'

More SCO19 officers ran in. Kane raised a hand. He wanted to saying something.

'You have my word,' Trent said.

The line crackled. Vondell breathed heavily. 'Me and Jackson. That's all it ever was. Tonight was meant to be. Woman or no woman.' The snarl returned. 'I'm hot. You get me in.'

'Not via the warm-up track. Not if Jackson's there. You see the sculpture? Across the bank.'

Trent had seen it driving in. Some art kind of installation, rainbow coloured, by the south perimeter.

'It's so dark here ... wait, I see it.'

'Ten minutes. I'll meet you with an armed escort. When I flash a torch, you come across the bridge.'

Kane dived over. He tried to grab Trent's phone, but Vondell had gone.

'We're solving a murder case!' Kane said, 'not fucking babysitting!'

'He's given us what we need: the time of the hit,' Trent said. 'Stocking pushed it back - right after de Witt's men fell out. It's all there on Schalk's phone.'

'Masterson thinks you're searching for Vondell,' Claire said. 'I'll keep her sweet. But if Rabbatts sticks his nose in I'll have to tell him the truth.' She looked into the arena. 'I'll keep watch on de Witt.'

Kane grimaced. He laced fingers behind his neck. 'Okay, okay. I'll phone Krentz and Chisolm. He stuck a finger in Trent's face. 'Like Masterson says - you better fucking be right!'

THIRTY

'Get out the way, I can't see!'

Friends and family of the competitors had bagged the first couple of rows around the bend. Trent ignored the protests and barged to the front. He spoke to a steward and positioned himself on the steps facing the start line. Beside him was Sid, a plainclothes SCO19 officer who'd helped to bring Vondell back in. If de Witt had another gunman, there was at least some chance of stopping him with Sid there. But there were 80,000 in the stadium. Preventing a lone wolf attack was nigh on impossible.

A fanfare heralded the finalists.

In lane three, representing the Netherlands, Gaston Slaider!

A large square of red carpet had been laid out by the organisers. The Dutchman strutted out to Crime Mob's *Knuck If You Buck*, the bass shuddering the stand. He stopped to arc his arms and pecs, his muscles bursting through his orange vest, then growled and wagged a finger at the camera.

Jackson was next. A roar greeted his name. The screen flashed through his greatest wins. A good ten seconds passed before he appeared. He was wearing black tights and a gold vest, waving regally but avoiding the camera directly. He seemed confident but distant. Nervous, even. Not a look Trent had seen before.

In lane five, representing Panama, two-time Pan-American champion and current world record holder, Darius Vondell!

A teenager to Trent's right leapt up and booed, sparking others to do the same. The Panamanian fans by the finish line shot up with their flags, whooping and punching the air. It was a two-horse race - that was evident - but there was no doubt whose side the crowd were on.

The lights zig-zagged over the carpet. The track on the PA was the same tinny number preceding each event. Vondell hadn't chosen it. The announcer threw out more career facts, but Vondell still didn't appear.

Officials with clipboards began to look at one another. The boy who'd booed was standing up with his friends, laughing and pointing at the screen.

Sid shifted, the sharp smell of his sweat catching in Trent's throat. The whole section where de Witt was sitting was now swathed in darkness.

Trent grabbed his phone. 'Claire, where's Vondell?!'

'Wait -' she yelled above the PA. 'Let me move -'

Trent dashed to the barrier. He'd delivered Vondell to the door of the locker room, leaving an armed guard outside. There was no way he could go AWOL again.

A slow hand clap rose from the back straight. Photographers rushed for a better view. Trent skirted around the ad hoardings, only to run into a team of stewards handing out water. One woman had fainted in the heat, and was being treated by the track.

'Claire! Where -'

The tinny intro restarted. Lights swarmed over the empty carpet.

Then he appeared. A black hoodie shrouded his face. Vondell stopped and turned, as if eyeballing each spectator in turn. Pockets of cheers erupted. He looked like one of de

Witt's fighters on a ring walk.

The cameraman darted forward. Vondell stuck a palm in his face. The boos started again, but were drowned out by a frenzy of belated cheers.

The show had begun.

The announcer introduced the other finalists. Jackson did a few practice starts then stood motionless, staring down his lane.

'Claire, you still on de Witt?' Applause broke from the far side. A high jumper had just gone clear. 'Claire! You still on de Witt?!'

The phone whined. 'Roger, sorry, it's so loud, yes, he's still there.'

Vondell filled the screen. The camera traced his snake tattoo. He jogged into a sprint, venturing further up the track than the others.

He stalked back, looking directly at Jackson, but the American was unmoved, oblivious to the tension in the stands. The line-up was announced again. Then they were called forward.

A face with a finger to its lips appeared on the big screen. The crowd fell silent. Trent peeled his shirt from his chest. He scanned around. Those not on their feet were already straining from their seats. Nothing mattered more than the next ten seconds.

Vondell sprang twice into the air. He shouted something before kneeling, then placed his arms wide apart, his shoulders almost filling the narrow lane. Finally he rested back, his head up, as if poised for attack.

Jackson settled last. He pumped each leg, placing his shoes softly on their blocks like they were made of eggshell. The camera zoomed in. He crossed himself twice before kissing Gaines' photo.

Sid's arm twitched. A discarded programme had dropped from the stand and was drifting around the bend.

Set.

Eighteen arms shot up like pistons. The crack of the gun followed, barely audible beneath the torrent of noise. At five metres Vondell was ahead. The runners shifted to their drive phase. Jackson's head lifted first. At forty metres he found his stride, overhauling the Jamaican to his left.

At half way he'd caught Vondell. The Panamanian gritted his teeth. He was full-left of his lane, almost touching Jackson as the American came by. Jackson led. His wrists dropped, his arms swinging in that smooth, matchless rhythm that had brought so much success.

The volume swelled, like an aircraft taking off. Vondell reacted. At seventy metres he accelerated.

Sid jabbed Trent's ribs, 'He's only having a look!'

Jackson tightened. Vondell was looking right at him. The American's face contorted, the muscles strung rigid around his tightening jaw. The textbook action faltered. Ten metres out, he began to overstride, straining for a line that would never come.

Seizing his chance, Vondell propelled himself onwards, his chest dragging him on like a runaway bull. Ten thousand phones flashed. Jackson lunged for the line, but it was all too late.

His face said it all.

Vondell had won.

Sid jumped up. He bawled something in Trent's ear, but it was impossible to hear. The stand shook as 80,000 cavorted in a deafening tumult. Vondell carried on running around the bend, punching the air and leaping like a fish. He thumped his chest, then ran back to the Panamanian fans, many of whom were in tears. They draped a flag around his shoulders, before he turned to the press gallery, shouting and throwing a fist.

Trent's pocket vibrated. It was Kane. 'Sir, you'll have to speak up -'

Kane cackled. 'He only went and did it then! And no bugger to shoot him down!'

A murmur went around as Vondell's winning time was confirmed. Almost two-tenths outside his world record. Jackson was eight hundredths behind, with Slaider a distant third.

But times were irrelevant. Vondell had beaten Jackson.

What wasn't meant to happen had happened.

'So I got hold of Krentz,' Kane shouted. 'Zimmerman's choked. He's only gone and given up de Witt!'

'What?!'

'Shat himself when they mentioned this Castillo. Saying zilch about the poisoning business, but they reckon he'll cough on the betting scam. Knows the system, don't he? Krentz says he'll gun for a plea bargain. Claim he was under duress. Dark forces and all that. Short sentence, identity change - he'll probably be out by next summer.'

'What about Chisolm?'

'I ain't heard nothing. Probably still in some bookies. Listen -' Sid moved down the stairwell. Vondell was being swamped by fans wanting selfies. 'That French bird - Annette. Statement's come back. Reckons some Russian geezer came into the office - right after that Bashin promo. Says she saw him looking at some map with Stocking. CCTV confirmed it. The twins too!'

Trent grabbed Sid. 'Russian? What did he look like?'

'Short. Tight top. Biceps like melons.'

'The MMA guy who'd tried to take Vondell out! It's got to be. That or the driver. They were confirming the time and place of the hit. Stocking knew Vondell was at the east London track. That's why she'd pushed it back!' Trent shot up the steps. 'Has Masterson -'

'I can't hear you, son!'

Jackson was ambling round the bend, hands on hips. He caught up with Vondell. The screen caught their embrace. The American whispered something in his ear. Vondell stepped back, his frown melting in the broiling heat. He held out his hand. They hugged. The crowd, still in a frenzy at Vondell's win, began to applaud. There was no way Jackson had orchestrated the hit. He was ruthless - on the track, in business - but he wasn't a killer. If he did know what de Witt was up to, he'd be too terrified to admit it.

'I said has Masterson -'

'Hold on -' Kane broke off. He was speaking to her. Trent heard Rabbatts chip in. He sounded hysterical. 'Look, you better get up here. Forensics have come back. They've found an email -'

'What email?'

'Some draft ... a letter Jad Gaines never sent. He overheard de Witt and Schalk.' He broke off again. Rabbatts was yapping away. 'Vondell couldn't be allowed to win. By any means necessary - that's what he heard. The poor guy wrote it all down. Petrified, he was.'

Gaines' anxiousness that night at the track. It explained it all. He might have been on Jackson's team, but he and Vondell went further back. He'd put rivalries aside. He wasn't going to stand by and see his friend hurt. And he'd died telling him the truth.

'I'm there in five,' Trent said. 'I'll leave Sid on Vondell.'

Claire rang before he could move.

'Claire, they've found an email - from Gaines -'

'He's gone.'

'What? Who has?'

'De Witt!'

Trent tore down the steps. He held a hand to the floodlights. The top section of seating was in darkness, but there was plenty of movement below as people clamoured for sight of the medalists.

Except where de Witt had been sitting.

The top rows were empty.

The group had gone.

'For fuck's sake, Claire, you were watching him!'

'I'm sorry!' She gulped. There was desperation in her voice. 'Vondell was mobbed ... I was watching him through

184

the binos. De Witt … they must have got him out!'

'Let me call Masterson.' Trent ran for the stairwell. An insider. No question. Schalk, his car and the Vectra were under guard.

'They won't risk the parking lot.' Claire was running. 'They'll take the south entrance into the mall. Or head to the A12.'

They had to have a car. The thuggish entourage might fancy their chances, but there was no way de Witt would flee on foot.

'Meet me on the bridge -' Trent dropped his phone. Jackson was on his haunches by the clock showing Vondell's winning time. He was looking into the VIP area. The suits were in raptures. Association members. Sponsor execs. But Jackson was fixed on one person. The only spectator not applauding. Dressed in a power suit.

Just like Berlin.

Stocking.

'Trent! I said, are you bringing Kane -'

'I need to get by … sorry …' Trent pushed along the row. 'Claire, there's something …' He stopped. Anger seethed. After all the calls. The phone traces. Some insider had sneaked her in. Why wasn't she with de Witt? Had she really come for this? A ringside seat for her boyfriend's execution?

He scrambled over bags and coats. Jackson was still panting, the image of Gaines pulsing on his chest.

Betrayal. Her look said it all. What she had done - what they had done - it didn't matter. Jackson had lost. There were no second chances.

Trent pulled Sid to the exit. A bottleneck blocked their way.

Claire buzzed again. Trent looked across the stadium. The spot where de Witt had sat gaped like a void. The bigger prize. Arrest him and they'd have Stocking. Schalk was in custody. Zimmerman had confessed. Take the South

185

African and they might even nail Castillo.

'Trent?!' Claire yelled. 'I need you!'

'I'll call Kane. The bridge in five!'

Stocking was standing, arms folded, her hair in a bun. He remembered how Schönleber had ogled her in Berlin. Her star had outshone Jackson's that night. Trent too had been blinded - but Gaines and the German had paid a far greater price.

He watched her pull her phone from her handbag. He remembered the hidden one in the penthouse. And what had happened next.

You should probably be going ...

He hesitated. No. Not again. Just a face in the crowd. That's all she was. He felt nothing. She was an accessory to murder. Rabbatts would take her in. Then it would end.

'Sir -'

'Get up here!' Kane barked. 'Gaines' email - Masterson's got the warrant. Culverhouse's about to give the arrest order.'

'De Witt's gone, sir - he's done a runner.'

'What?! I thought Claire was on him!?' Kane bawled something at Rabbatts. 'Trent, you -'

'Stocking's here. Fifty feet below your box. The VIP seats.'

'Shit the -'

'Get Rabbatts to bring her in. Tell Masterson we're going after de Witt. Claire's giving chase. She's in danger -'

'Flaming nora ... where's Bad Boy?'

Vondell was on his lap of honour, posing and signing autographs.

'Sid's on him. He's sound.'

'Jesus ...' Kane came to the ops room window. Masterson, Culverhouse and Rabbatts were squabbling in the background. On foot Kane was slow. It'd be quicker with just him and Claire. But Trent needed him.

He always did.

186

'Okay. Leave Masterson to me.' Kane lowered his voice. 'Rabbatts has a pool tractor. We're taking it. That's one-up on the Saffa, right off. And I'm driving!'

THIRTY-ONE

'You blagged this?!' Claire wrenched open the rear door. 'How!?'

Kane reached onto the Range Rover's back seat. He swatted aside his briefcase. 'Rabbatts' junior. I pulled rank. Now get in!'

The car was white but unmarked. The spit of de Witt's. The irony. Cuffing him in the back seat. Like a common criminal. Kane was relishing it. He'd never even met the guy, but he knew a spiv when he saw one. Managers. Promoters. They were all the same.

Trent pulled up the satnav. 'So south gate security saw nothing? Is there any other way out?'

'Nope,' Claire said. 'Not without crossing the lake. And I don't see de Witt swimming.'

They were parked on the bridge. Below them the stadium lights shimmered in the black water.

The transit exit by the mall was on lockdown. It wasn't an option. A drop-off, then escape on foot. It had to be. Whoever had smuggled them in had got them out. The only other route was the A12, but the approach by the media hub was exposed - armed guards at the barriers would see them a mile off.

'The mall.' Kane slammed into reverse. 'They have to be there.'

Trent checked the mirror. A van with no lights on was coming the other way.

'Slow down,' he said.

'Eh?'

'I said slow down.' The van passed. 'Who was driving? Did you see who was driving?!'

'No -'

'Claire?'

'I didn't see!'

The dark blue transit carried on towards the stadium. It drove under a streetlight. There were two in the front, Trent saw, the driver and a passenger. Beyond them, a pair of orange-bibbed stewards were chatting by a road block. One made a stop sign. The other signalled for the driver to wind his window. The van slowed. The second steward walked over.

'A contractor van?' Claire said.

'It's too dark,' Trent said. 'I can't see the name -'

The left door of the van shot open, sending the steward sprawling on the tarmac. With a roar, it shot forward, snaking left and right before crashing through the bollards.

'It's him!' Trent shouted. 'Go!'

'We don't know it's de Witt!' Claire said.

Kane put his foot down. 'They ain't here to fix a leak. Hold on!'

The other steward dived for cover. The van skidded right at the corner and headed for the media hub.

Trent grabbed the dashboard. They screeched around the bend, almost on two wheels.

Kane's driving: you were safer outside than in.

'We're losing them!' Claire shouted.

A megaphone parped a warning. Lights burst from the carriageway exit where Trent had first spied the Vectra.

Squad cars were lined up on the verge, the road barred with concrete blocks.

'They'll stop 'em at the checkpoint!' Kane roared. 'You'd need a tank to get through!'

They raced by the TV studios. The van hurtled along the park's edge, gaining speed towards the barrier.

'They're armed!' Trent cried.

Three sentries manned the checkpoint. They ran forward, gesturing frantically for the van to stop. When it didn't, they raised their guns.

STOP THE CAR. THIS IS A POLICE WARNING -

The van jackknifed, the howl of tires drowning out the megaphone. The armed officers dived for cover. Dodging the security blocks, it mounted the kerb and headed straight for an ad hoarding.

'Shit the bed!'

A young couple beamed from the giant billboard. The van smashed into the bottom-right corner, flipping it over like a playing card. It bounced once over some rubble, before bursting through a gate and out onto the carriageway.

'Get down!' Trent shoved Kane's head onto the steering wheel. The armed men had recovered and were standing wide-eyed in their lights, their barrels trained right on them. Police and security were scrambling everywhere.

Kane yanked the wheel to avoid more orange bibs, then swung onto the grass. They shot under the now horizontal hoarding, ripping the hanging gate from its hinges.

Red lights streamed up the flyover. Cars swerved as Kane scythed through the traffic. Seconds later they were in the fast lane.

'Why didn't they shoot?!' Claire shouted, breathing hard. 'They could have shot us!'

'This ain't fucking America!' Kane shifted gear.

'There!' Trent pointed up the hill.

The van lurched left as it climbed, almost crushing a

motorcyclist. Behind it the stadium honed back in view, its white halo scorching the night.

Sirens rang out. Trent glanced in the mirror. Blue lights. Lots of them.

'The cavalry, thank God.' Kane glanced up. 'It's Rabbatts.'

'What?'

'You can't do it all, my son. However much you want inspector.'

Trent craned around. Squad cars and an unmarked Volvo were burning up behind.

'I told him to follow.' Kane passed Trent his radio. 'Sid and his men too. Now get that plate number to Masterson.'

'Where is she?'

'With Rabbatts. Come on!'

You'd better be right. Masterson's words rang in Trent's ears. Kane might have stolen Rabbatts' car, but he'd been sure to tell her where he was going. Trent wondered if even Kane trusted his theory.

'Superintendent Masterson.'

'Ma'am. It's Trent. We've eyes on de Witt. I've got the plate -'

'Vondell's under guard,' she replied. 'Culverhouse's trying to bring Jackson in too.'

Trent released the dashboard. So she was all-in. Rabbatts was chuntering in the background, but it seemed Culverhouse was onboard as well. Now he had to deliver.

He read the van's number.

'How many inside?' Masterson said.

'Two up front. De Witt's in the back. He has to be. His muscle ... I'm not sure. There were more in the stadium. They can't all have disappeared.'

A car transporter honked as Kane cut him up.

'We need to know where he's heading,' Masterson said. 'If he turns off we could stinger the road. There's the airport ... but they may switch rides.'

191

'He's due in Munich,' Trent said. 'Drey-Bashin. He's left it late, but if there's a private jet -'

Rabbatts said something in the background. 'Tell Kane to get in closer. We need an ID on that driver.'

Signs to Docklands streamed overhead. The same route Gaines had driven. How long had he stewed on that email? The guy had felt alone. That much was clear. Jackson claimed he'd been like a brother. What kind of brother, forensics would find out.

The van, still with no lights on, jumped across to the slow lane before careering back behind a taxi. Kane dodged in behind. They were slowing. New apartments in various states of completion loomed, each rooftop studded with red safety lights.

Claire popped up. 'These syndicates. How do they work? I mean, de Witt, Castillo - if they're such big operations, how do they keep all the money coming in? It'd be like herding cats.'

'Fear. Extortion. Come on!' Kane thumped the horn. The traffic was building before the underpass. 'It's a tax. Protection money. Local overlords make sure everyone pays up. The money transfers into microbets to escape government and the tax man. Reverse laundering. Bookmakers in on it, too. Dirty money gets proper filthy. Your big bosses like Castillo never see a chit. Neither do big shots like de Witt - unless they're too greedy or stupid to keep out the game -'

'The underpass!' Trent said. 'We're losing them!'

Bromley-by-Bow station zipped passed. The van dived into the tunnel, jinking left and right as the sirens closed in. Kane swept over to the wall, tracking the van underground.

'I'll get up beside,' he said. 'See which bugger's driving.' He slammed his foot down.

'Sir, watch out!' The van slipped between two HGVs, making them shudder violently. Kane braked. Outside the tunnel line traffic was stacking up at a junction.

'Damn it, come on!' Trent smacked the window. Behind them Masterson and the wall of blue were blocked.

Kane edged out. He picked his way through. The van, frustrated by the jam, was flashing its lights and tailgating. Finally freeing itself, it swung left up East India Dock Road.

'City Airport,' Trent said. 'It has to be.'

His phone rang. Masterson again.

'Trent, they're trying for City Airport. We -'

He stuck a finger in his ear. The convoy of police vehicles was right behind, sirens blaring.

'Sorry, ma'am - go ahead.'

'We'll ground all outbound flights.' She gave the order to Rabbatts. 'Wait, he's slowing!'

The road narrowed. The van crawled between some abandoned units. A sweet, burning smell rose between the brick walls. The sugar factory, Trent guessed.

'What's he up to?' Kane lagged back. 'Where's he going -' The van pulled in, disappearing between a line of parked trucks. 'What is that place?'

Trent stuck his head out the window. 'Council depot by the looks of it. Hold on -'

Tyres screeched. The van accelerated out of the layby, then shot off once more.

'There he is - go!' They flew past the trucks. 'What the -' Trent swivelled. Two men in bomber jackets ran out from behind a parked car. The pair dragged out a dumpster and hurled it at an oncoming squad car, causing it to swerve and crash into a truck. One of the assailants, a scarf around his face, then found a shopping trolley and launched it at the windshield of the car behind. It bounced off the glass, striking the next vehicle in pursuit.

Four uniformed officers jumped out. The attackers ran for the depot, but were leapt on by the gate.

Kane swerved to avoid a wall. 'What was all that?!'

'De Witt's muscle.'

'How many are in there?!'

193

'He's getting away!' Claire shouted.

They sped on past the sugar factory.

'Trent? Trent!' It was Masterson.

'Sorry ma'am, I'm still here.'

'We're stuck behind - what's happened?!'

He explained.

'We've alerted airport security,' she said. 'Rabbatts is sorting the planes.'

'What about Stocking?' He'd almost forgotten. Locked in an interview room, he hoped. Well away from Jackson. And Vondell. 'Sorry ma'am, you're breaking up -' The radio stuttered. 'Ma'am?' He rapped it on the dashboard. The forest of new apartments was dashing the signal.

'This'll be fun,' Kane braced himself. 'Hold on!'

A pop-up market had sprung up by a high-rise. The drinkers scattered as the van accelerated. Veering at the last moment, it clouted a trestle table, showering the hipsters in a vat of pulled pork.

Kane swerved a burrito stall.

'Prick!' A drinker thumped their hood. Kane dodged the broken glass. Up ahead, the van was entering the docks.

'Come on ...' Trent slammed the glove box. 'Where's Masterson? The others?'

Claire looked round. 'No sight. They must still be held up.'

The van entered Silvertown. The docks glowed orange in the streetlights, the airport terminal burning through the haze. They passed under the monorail and over the river. Planes were lined up on the apron. The van skidded at the roundabout and headed straight toward them.

'They're going around the back,' Trent said. 'There's no entrance there.'

Kane took a left. 'So they ain't rollin' out the red carpet, then?'

Sirens. Trent glanced around. Blue lights were steaming up Victoria Dock Road.

'It's SCO19.'

'Thank Christ,' Kane said. The van flew up a service road by the perimeter fence. They gave chase by the river's edge. 'He's not ... wait ... no, he is!'

A barrier blocked the road. Beside it was an unmanned cabin. The van smashed through, sending the yellow arm spiralling into the Thames.

Trent ducked as the stub ripped off their mirror.

'They're heading for the freight park!'

THIRTY-TWO

The gate was open. The van hit a ramp, bounced once and shrieked to a halt.

The driver and passenger, their faces covered, jumped out. An arm groped from the rear door. Then a leg. Desperate to get away the men reached in and dragged the struggling passenger out.

De Witt blinked into Kane's lights. His accomplices turned their backs.

Black bomber jackets.

The same beanie hats.

The guys who'd chased Gaines to his death.

It was all coming back. Kane ran for the van. De Witt was already halfway across the tarmac, being dragged on by the Russians. Seeing Kane in pursuit, Nikolai ran back. Kane raised an arm but the Russian was onto him. He punched him in the belly, sending Kane crumpling to the ground.

The sirens were closing in. Trent kicked open the Range Rover door. Behind him Claire was hammering at the window, unable to get out.

Nikolai aimed a boot at Kane's head. Kane pulled him

to the ground. Trent dived onto the Russian and hauled him off. The first police car roared in, its lights swathing Nikolai's scars in blue. He shouted something but Sid was already on him, bending his arm back and frisking him for weapons.

Claire had managed to get free and threw herself face-down on the fighter's legs.

'Just this?!' Sid wrenched a knife from Nikolai's pocket. He bawled something in Russian. Sid pushed his face to the dirt. 'Where they going? Where the others going?!' He shouted to Kane but was drowned out by a plane taking off.

'I thought they'd been grounded!' Trent shouted.

'Seems like they ain't!' Kane rubbed his stomach.

'You ok?'

'There!' Kane pointed. Someone in the shadows was holding open a gate.

It was Sergei. He and De Witt exchanged words then forced their way through. Trent ran between the parked trucks, catching the gate as it shut. A stadium-sized hangar separated them from the terminal. Ignoring the trespass warnings, they clambered over a stack of pallets to see De Witt and Sergei disappear inside.

The ramp of a giant cargo plane gaped open. Three or four more sat like beached whales under the fluorescent lights. There was no sign of any staff.

'Where'd they go?!' Kane ran up the plane's ramp.

The background generators were deafening. Trent stuck his fingers in his ears. They searched the plane. Some boxes lay piled at the back, but nothing else.

They picked their way through the forklifts. The second plane was loaded with roll cages stuffed with parcels. Kane took out a package. Holding it up, he grinned.

LARGE INSTRUMENT - HANDLE WITH CARE

A cage shot forward. The impact pitched Kane over the ramp's edge. A knife lunged from the shadows. Sergei hurled a cage at Trent, striking him in the temple and flooring him on the incline.

Trent blinked. A blade stabbed down. He rolled away, falling three feet onto the hangar tiles.

Pain gripped his ribs. He scrambled to his knees as Sergei ran around. The Russian swung again, but Trent's weight was already spearing his attacker's waist. With a groan Sergei fell back, hitting his head on a forklift's mast.

Trent's chest throbbed. He grabbed Sergei's wrist and smashed it against the metal. The Russian's fist tightened around the knife. Trent grabbed his throat. They rolled onto the concrete. Sergei thrashed his knife hand free, slashing Trent in the abdomen.

Trent cried out in pain. A burning gripped his side. He fought to get free, clubbing a fist in Sergei's face. The Russian howled. He fell back, his hand to his nose, blood streaming down his cheek.

'Give it up!' An arm appeared around Sergei's neck. Kane clasped him in a headlock and wrenched the knife away, sending it scuttling under a plane.

Trent went to pin his arms, only for the Russian to kick out again. The force freed him from Kane's hold. He swept Trent's legs away, throwing them into a cage fight grapple.

More sirens. Sergei knelt on Trent, his face covered with blood. He grabbed Trent by the throat. Kane jumped on his back as voices filled the hangar.

'De Witt!' Trent said, gagging on Sergei's nicotine fingers. 'Find ... de Witt ...'

Sid ran in. He threw Kane aside and stuck his rifle in Sergei's ear.

'Off!' He dragged the Russian away.

Sergei bawled something.

'Shut it!' Kane bound his wrists.

'Where's his mate?' Trent said, rubbing his neck.

'In the wagon,' said Sid. Two more SCO19 ran in and dragged Sergei away. 'Masterson's out there with Claire. Rabbatts too.' He saw Kane walking off. 'Whoa - where you going?'

'De Witt. He's in here somewhere.'

'What's that?' Sid said, seeing blood on Trent's shirt.

'A scratch.' Trent felt the wound. It was a graze, nothing deep. He hauled Kane away. 'Come on!'

The third plane was loaded with food bound for the Far East. As they searched the hold, the hangar alarm went off. Trent rifled through the cages. Security were on their way. With a bit of luck de Witt might run straight into them, but Trent wouldn't be giving them the pleasure.

Kane opened the cockpit door. Nothing.

'The insider,' he said, shaking his head. 'De Witt could have -'

A clang rang out from the terminal end. They ran down the steps. A tube of metal sheeting rolled across the floor. Behind it, something flashed between the pallet stacks.

'There!' Trent pointed.

Kane forced his way through. 'It's him!'

De Witt disappeared over a tarpaulin. They climbed over the boxes and slid through.

'Police, give it up!' Kane slipped on the metal sheeting, swearing and nursing his leg.

The giant hangar doors were closing.

'He's trapped, sir,' Trent said. 'Slow down!'

'No way. I want that droopy-'tached Buddha in the meat wagon, right now. Come on!' Kane clutched his knee. He clambered over more boxes. At the top of a ramp he pointed, but it was impossible to hear above the alarm.

They ran down the steps. Orange warning lights were flashing above the sliding door. De Witt was limping too, and making for the terminal.

They weaved between some freezer containers.

'It's over!' Trent shouted. 'We have your Russians!'

De Witt stopped. They could hear him wheeze. He bent over and held his leg.

'Schalk,' Trent said. 'We've taken him in. The sniper rifle

199

too. The betting scam - we know it all.'

The hangar door was almost shut. De Witt snatched a cage. He swung it backwards, only to trip as he ran.

The doors met with a deadened clank.

'No, God damn you!' He slammed his fists against the steel. Trent tore him off. The South African wrestled free, his face the colour of a running track.

Trent slammed him against a freezer crate. De Witt stumbled back, falling heavily into the containers.

'Get me up! Get me up! I'm fucking freezing!' A lid fell free. He pawed into the ice, yelping at his hand touched something sharp. The box was full of crabs, flown in from the Philippines. 'You'll pay for this! All of you! Don't you know who I am?'

Trent ripped out his badge. 'I'm arresting you for the murder of Jad Gaines and the attempted murder of Darius Vondell -'

'You!' De Witt jabbed a swollen finger. 'I know you! Ya, believe me, you're in a whole fucking world of shit.'

Trent read him his rights.

Kane arrived, panting. 'Making friends, is he?'

'Who the fuck are you?' De Witt said.

'Gary Cooper, now turn round.' They cuffed him to the cage.

'Culverhouse,' de Witt huffed. 'The big boss. You get me him. Now. Or his bunny, Rabbatts.'

Trent looked at Kane. The insider. Surely not Rabbatts …

Trent searched de Witt's pockets. 'Keep it for the courtroom. Zimmerman's choked. We've a trail back to the Far East.'

He heard Sid shout. The others were coming.

'You don't know shit!' De Witt spat. 'You're a tench. A fucking floor feeder.' Another box had split. Trent slammed de Witt's face into the ice. He bellowed like a crippled ox, the echo bouncing from the walls.

'Trent!' Masterson ran in. She pulled him off. Behind her were Sid and Rabbatts.

De Witt's face said nothing. Either he'd never met Rabbatts or he was hiding it well.

'A woman!' De Witt belly-laughed. 'Fucking hell ...'

'Get him up!' Masterson said. Kane did as he was told. The alarm went off again. The doors started to open. Outside, the terminal was emptying, the gates barred with security cords.

Claire ran in with the other armed men. A custody van arrived outside.

'You're making one huge fucking mistake.' De Witt stuck his face in Masterson's. His moustache was crusted with ice, like fat on a day-old roast. 'You've no right -'

'Our warrant says otherwise. Take him in.'

'Fine.' De Witt raised his hands. 'Fine! We'll do it your way. My lawyer's in town.' He sniggered. 'I might even make Munich.' He bumped Masterson aside.

She flicked her shoulder. 'Let's hope Castillo's as forgiving.'

De Witt stopped. 'What?'

'Castillo. His justice is of a less ... formal kind, one suspects.'

De Witt gripped a rollcage, his eyes bulging. 'I don't know who -'

'You'll lead us right to him. If he doesn't get you first.'

'These syndicates,' Kane said. 'They don't do losing. And it's amazing who - or what - they smuggle into jails ...'

The colour drained from de Witt's face. Trent thought of von Schrader in his garden, looking out across the sand flats, where they'd once prepared the bomb.

De Witt's wrists were shaking. He tried to stand but his legs buckled.

'My lawyer!' He grappled with the armed men. 'I want my lawyer!'

Masterson opened the van. 'Get him in.'

'Is Drey-Bashin fixed too?' Kane shouted. 'Hope not, 'cos I've got a pony on it.'

'No!' De Witt lashed out. The officers grabbed a limb each. 'What they'll do ... you don't understand -'

'Stocking!' Trent turned to Masterson. He'd almost forgotten. 'He's not told us about Gabrielle Stocking! She was there - in the stand -'

De Witt starfished himself against the van's open doors. There was a blind terror in his eyes, like a condemned man. Ignoring his pleas, the officers chopped his arms away and bundled him in like laundry.

'Leave it.' Masterson pulled Trent away. 'We've got enough.'

A hand touched Trent's side.

'You're hurt,' Claire said.

He felt the sticky blood. 'Looks worse than it is.'

'I've spoken to Lester.'

Rabbatts was talking earnestly with Masterson. The stadium insider. It couldn't be ...

'Jay, I said I've spoken to Nick Lester -'

Trent butted in. 'Excuse me, ma'am.' Rabbatts was looking pleased with himself, as if he'd just narrated some great victory. 'Rabbatts - you never met de Witt, right? Not before just now.'

'Nah, mate. I was just saying to Superintendent Masterson here: without the forensics on Schalk we'd never have reeled him in -'

The rest dissolved in a swirl of background noise. For once, he wasn't bullshitting. For all the phoney banter, a careerist like Rabbatts was as straight a die. He'd sell his mother before risking his job.

'Say Frank -' Rabbatts tapped Kane's hip. 'You got a pony on Drey-Bashin?! Who'd you back?'

Kane rolled his eyes. 'The Yank.'

'Fifty notes on Drey!'

'Twenty-five, you cock.'

Trent hadn't finished. 'You haven't mentioned Stocking - you were meant to pick her up -'

'She's an accessory.' Rabbatts grinned at Masterson. 'We've taken down Maureece de Witt! It's all about the big picture, yeah? And it don't get much bigger than this.'

Masterson hesitated. 'He's right, Trent. She won't be going far. Not with de Witt and Schalk under arrest.'

A golf cart arrived loaded with airport security. They blinked around the hangar, oblivious to what had just happened. Sid filled them in and waved off the van. Rabbatts had delved into an ice box and was pretending to scare Kane with a crab.

Claire tugged Trent aside. 'She's been calling the Far East,' she whispered. 'Lester's back up on the trace.'

'What?' Trent said. One of the security staff had switched on a humidifier, amplifying the din. 'Can someone turn that thing off?!'

'KL. Manila. A dozen times this evening.'

'What?! Are you sure?'

'When's Lester ever been wrong?'

He ran across the apron. Heat from the runway fizzed above the landing lights. To the far side of the scrub a small jet was swivelling in a silent ballet, its red wing lights like rubies in the dark.

'I thought -' He turned to Claire. 'What's the number? Give me your phone!'

As they scanned the call list his pocket vibrated.

Number unknown.

The jet was taxiing to the runway.

She needed to share.

Claire threw up her arms, pointing and swearing at the control tower.

Trent took her hand. 'It's -'

'I know.' She pulled away. 'Just go.'

THIRTY-THREE

'So who was it?' Trent swapped phone hands. 'The insider? Who got you in?'

Stocking spoke with someone. Glasses clinked. He thought he heard laughter.

'Sergeant Trent. So conspicuous out there. All alone, trespassing on airport property. An offence in itself, is it not?'

Her voice. Each word cut his flesh. A set of cabin stairs lay marooned between the plane holding pads. He side-stepped beneath them, as if hiding from his conscience.

'Oh,' she went on, 'and don't think about running. There's a rifle trained on your forehead. Your colleagues too.'

The plane had stopped. Back at the hangar Claire was arguing with Kane and Masterson. The SCO19 guys were joking with security, high-fiving over a drink.

'You won't get away. We've a trail. Right back to de Witt - and beyond.' He explained it all. The time of the botched hit. Schalk's phone, his frantic calls with the Russian. How Annette and the twins had confirmed Sergei's visit to her office, the whole thing caught on camera.

She laughed. 'Remarkable! "Inspector Trent". I see now why you're so keen.'

'So it's all true?'

'I wouldn't go that far.'

'You cheated on your boyfriend in order to kill his rival. What you've done - don't you realise? Jad Gaines is dead.'

'One moment -' She spoke to someone. 'Yes, such a tragedy. And him so young -' She broke off again. Did he hear a sniff? 'Just don't crucify Lemond, ok? He's a puppy, behind all the ego stuff. I could tell you he knows nothing, but you wouldn't believe me anyway -'

'Then why does he look so terrified? Every time I mention de Witt?'

'Maureece is, let's say, somewhat demanding of his clients.'

'Meaning?'

She sighed. 'Lemond Jackson's received a great deal of investment from de Witt Associates. A *lot* more than some of our fighters, believe me. But the race fees he commands … his image rights … as a return on investment they just don't add up. The Learjet: did you know it's on rental? With penalties for late return! Lemond couldn't buy one if he had won tonight.'

'So you all fancied a cut? A windfall from this betting scam? To make up the shortfall?'

'Hmm ..' She purred. 'Lemond thinks he's smart. He likes nice things, too, but he doesn't do complex arrangements.'

Complex arrangements? 'So that's why he shits a brick when he hears de Witt's name? Money?'

'Partly. He's a control freak. That's great for a watch commercial, a sponsorship deal. But he doesn't know when to stop.' She paused. Impatiently, she said, 'He needs to learn … he needs to keep his mouth shut -'

'So he did know about Vondell, the grand plan -'

'No! I told you. It's -' Her voice was more insistent. 'It

205

was Gaines. He was acting oddly. Lemond asked too many questions. They were spending too much time alone.'

Jackson's tears over Gaines were sincere - Trent had never doubted that. But it hadn't stopped him suspecting the American's wider involvement.

'So Jackson had to win tonight ... or else?'

'Jason! You're putting words into my mouth.'

Her tone thawed. He remembered her in the Monaco penthouse. Standing in the doorway. She was doing the same now. Enjoying it. Reeling him in. Tethering the leash.

Him. Schönleber. Now Jackson too. At least Vondell was safe under guard. It was the American Trent was most worried about. True, he had his own "good people", but they were on De Witt's payroll too. What if one of them -

A low rumble rose to a crescendo, then died away. Across the field the plane rolled forward from the shadows.

Trent ventured into the scrub by the runway.

'Why tell me all this? You do realise I'm a police officer?'

'There's something else you should know.' She broke off again. More voices.

He remembered Vondell's words:

She'd look out for me ... and I believed that crap.

'How could you?' Trent said. 'Lead them into a honey trap - both of them - with Jad Gaines caught inbetween?'

'You don't understand - what happened in Berlin - It was never meant to go further.'

'The poisoning?'

'I only agreed ... Maureece assured me. No long term health damage. The official's complaint, engineering that was my idea, okay, I admit it, but the spiking was all de Witt. I swear, to that point I'd never ... Look, I'm saying too much.' She swallowed. 'I said there's something you need to hear -'

'You haven't answered my question.' She didn't need to. She couldn't help herself. Status. Money. They were the same thing to her. He'd remembered enough psychology to see through the facade. She needed to share. To be defined by others. Her crime was her achievement. And she was sharing it with the one person it might impress.

'That night in Monte Carlo ...' Her tone was softer, warmer. He could see her lips moving. 'When you came up to the suite ... what did you really want?'

'Your whereabouts. You and Jackson. The night before Berlin.'

She giggled. 'Not sure I answered that. Guess we were too distracted?'

The nape of her neck. How she swept her hair back. Her weight as she came down on him ...

A haze of kerosene drifted over from the plane. He retreated coughing under the steps.

'So that's all it was?' he said, 'Fortune and profile? How about your book sales? I'm sure there's plenty to be made there.' A boy growing up in poverty. Trust in an older woman. Their unlikely relationship. He didn't need his psychology to know where she'd filched *that* plot from. She'd almost stolen Vondell's future, and was happy to flay his past.

'Look, I fall for people okay?' She was angry again. 'Believe me, I care deeply about Lemond.'

'You've a funny way of showing it.'

'With Darius ... it just happened. You won't believe that either, but there was a truth to what we had.'

'Right until you decided to kill him.'

'He ...' Her voice cracked. 'He gets so angry -' She sniffed. 'The first time I forgave him - I mean, when he hit me. When it happened again ... I told de Witt ... from then ... right after his world record - it got so out of control.'

'But you were photographed. In Hyde Park.'

She laughed. 'The fool! What he was promising ... how we'd start over together. He'd retire after the Olympics. Start a fashion line. We'd go back to Panama. There's a

207

house he's building there.'

'Sounds idyllic.'

'He's nothing! Even after tonight. Sponsors won't touch him. He's a wrecking ball.' She sounded disgusted. 'I nearly lost it all before. After Jeff died. When you've lived a certain way ...' The plane fired up. It was moving to the taxiway. 'I won't. Go back. Again.'

Trent ran to the tarmac. If there was a sniper he'd be dead by now. Claire had pulled in the armed officers and was gesturing towards the plane. A solitary figure in the control tower looked out with binoculars. Trent wanted to raise the alarm but was unable to move, as if the heat had melted the ground.

'Why me? The auction invite. You tracked me down -'

'Better inside the camp than out. That was my call. De Witt wanted you thrown from the TV tower.'

He mopped his brow.

'And these Germans. So damned clever. Having the boy, Schönefeld - whatever his name is - follow you. Carl Zimmerman's idea. Though neither of them can keep their mouth shut, either.'

Trent couldn't help but smile. There was something comic about the bluster of de Witt's operation and their inept use of technology - twentieth century criminals in a digital world. Somewhere in the rag-tag operation of socialites, gangsters and thugs, a smart criminal machine waited to be fired up. Stocking was the spark. The real intelligence. De Witt might shudder at the thought of Castillo, but how much had he trusted her?

Someone shouted. The golf buggy was speeding towards the runway. Kane was at the wheel. Beside him were Masterson and Claire, the SCO19 guys perched like assault troops on the back.

'They'll come for you,' Trent said. 'Castillo ... we've got evidence back to Asia. You fucked up. These people don't forgive.'

'I don't know who you mean.'

The jet turned ninety degrees. Blinds covered the windows. A light was on.

'Castillo. The overlord. Owns every sports official south of Hong Kong.'

'Hong Kong? I love the Far East. You know, people make so many false assumptions about different cultures. They really should travel more.'

The plane accelerated to the far end of the runway. Trent ran between the edge lights. He turned to the control tower, waving frantically at the lone figure. Blue lights filled the freight park as more squad cars screamed in.

He remembered his promise to Vondell. Learn the truth about Berlin. He'd done that. But he wouldn't be calling him up. Not now. Not after what Stocking had said about him assaulting her. The Panamanian would have his gold medal tomorrow. He would make do with that.

Besides, hell knows what he'd do if told the truth.

'Gabby?!' The call was still active. 'Gabby?!'

He sprinted up the tarmac. The plane had reached the start of the runway. It stopped and swivelled to face him.

'Gabrielle? Are you there?!'

The plane shimmered like a mirage in the lights.

'This is crazy. Whoever's been bribed - air traffic, stadium security - you won't get away with it. You'll be tracked on radar -'

'It's too late,' she said. 'It's my turn now. I said there's something you should hear.'

Someone shouted his name. Kane was careering up the runway, the buggy bouncing over the central strip.

He's doping.

Who is?

Del Rey.

Trent heard his own voice. He pressed his phone to his ear.

Forget it, it's history. There's bigger fish to fry.

209

'Hold on,' she said. 'Just a little more ...'

But the doctor - he's a big shot now. Running a cartel. You could make a case - this could be big.

I won't tell if you won't. More whisky?

'Concealing evidence. Sleeping with a suspect. Abuse of police privilege in general.' She relaxed again. 'You can probably add misappropriation of police funds, but there's more than enough to see you fired, with a jail sentence to boot. There'll be no Inspector Trent. You'll be joining de Witt. In a cell. With all the other rank amateurs.'

TURN OFF THE ENGINES AND AWAIT POLICE BOARDING. YOU ARE NOT CLEARED FOR TAKE-OFF ...

The megaphone repeated the warning. Trent held his damaged rib. What she'd said in Mick's café, her threat, how she'd wreck his career. She'd come good on her promise. He'd delivered de Witt. The bigger prize. Or so he'd thought. But this was the blowback. He'd taken his eye off the ball.

He ran for the plane. 'Just tell me where you're going. We can work something out!'

An armada of police and security joined the runway. The jet's engines ignited, shuddering Trent's bowel. The roar flung him back, the nose of the aircraft bowing as it set off.

'Castillo!' he yelled. 'He'll come for you! The trail you've left ... we know everything. We can protect you. Just tell us where you're going!'

'I heard -' She gulped. The plane shot forward. 'I heard the Far East's nice ... at this time of year!'

Masterson came over the loud hailer. She ordered him aside. The men behind her jumped out and assumed firing positions, but they were never going to shoot.

This wasn't America.

'Goodbye, Sergeant Trent.'

The wings shook under turbulence. He dived to his chest. The plane's fuselage dipped, missing him by feet, then scythed through the convoy, sending squad cars skidding over the grass.

He covered his ears. The jet cleared the terminal, then with a groan banked northwards, pitching high above the stadium's roof, like a nighthawk from a trap.

ACKNOWLEDGEMENTS

Thanks to Lisa Grundberg, Andrew Granger, Chris Bates, Maxine Hitchcock, David Cheshire, Nick Bates, Tom Gash and Lucy Killick for their feedback and advice during the writing of this book.

Cover design: Chris Bates/Dreamstime

ABOUT THE AUTHOR

Chris Danson was born in Leicestershire and educated in York and Leeds. After a spell teaching English, he worked in digital publishing for national newspaper and advertising groups.

He is the author of *Dead in 10*, the first novel in the Jay Trent crime thriller series. He lives in London.

Visit www.chrisdanson.com

Follow Chris @dansonbooks:

twitter.com/dansonbooks
instagram.com/dansonbooks
facebook.com/dansonbooks

Printed in Poland
by Amazon Fulfillment
Poland Sp. z o.o., Wrocław